WITH KILLER VIEWS

CEECEE JAMES

For my Family

FOREWORD

Stella O'Neil has found a treasure of a house to list... a house possibly full of treasure, that is. Her new listing belonged to a man who died from a seemingly innocent accident. He also was embroiled in a bank investigation involving missing property and many enemies. The rumors have gone wild and people will stop at nothing to search it out.

If keeping treasure hunters out of her listing and avoiding being killed wasn't enough drama, Stella has finally found her mom and a way to rescue her. With the rest of her family in place, and the neighbor and a hunky policeman friend to help, she's determined to get her mom out. But someone is just as determined to stop her, even through murder.

Stella has come this far fighting to unite her family. She won't stop until she's finished. But will she regret it?

1

A gritty rumble advanced down the street and vibrated the floor boards under my feet. Inside my mug, the coffee's surface shivered like it was the skin of a cocoon about to peel off. I tensed, ready to spring for safety under the coffee table. This had to be the beginning of some crazy earthquake.

But an earthquake in Pennsylvania? How common was that? I decided there had to be something else going on, despite the fact that I wasn't an east coast earthquake expert. After all, I was from Seattle.

The growling grew louder and now carried the unmistakable bite of a car's engine. With a smile, I jumped up. I knew exactly what it was.

Jumped might be a small exaggeration. My foot was still

encased in a walking boot after weeks of being in a cast. I stumped over to the front door and flung it open.

As if racing the cloud of dust swelling behind it, a purple Challenger roared up the road at a breakneck speed.

Finally! Richie was bringing that sweet car over to give me my long promised ride. I tugged on a sneaker and then slammed the door behind me, before carefully picking my way down the steps to meet him.

He skidded into the driveway, tires spitting a wave of gravel. Casually, he rolled down the window and leaned out. His cowboy hat was pushed back off his suntanned forehead and his eyes twinkled. "You want a lift?"

"Uh, yeah!" I yelled back, already shambling over to the hot rod's passenger door. Did he have to ask twice? This was my dream car, honestly the one I'd hoped to get for myself when I first saw it at the dealership so long ago.

It turned out to be a good thing that I hadn't because money had been tight ever since then. Still, I'd been dying for a ride.

I sank into the vinyl bucket seat and slammed the heavy door behind me. The pebbled dash was perfect, and the silver chrome gleamed. Richie had done a fabulous job restoring it.

"How's your leg?" he asked, his forehead hitching up with concern.

"Almost completely healed," I answered optimistically. The last x-ray I had showed all the pins and screws had done their job and I was about to be set free from this final stage of immobilization. Those first weeks with the crutches about killed me. I had no idea you could develop callouses in your armpits.

"Terrific. Now, you buckled in?" He slipped into a lazy grin, his eyebrow arching innocently as if he didn't plan to knock my socks off.

I clicked the lap belt and gave it a yank, then nodded. He thumped the gear into reverse and stepped on the gas. Immediately the tires bit into the dirt. Positraction, baby. I giggled in anticipation of the wild ride.

He spun us out of the driveway and slammed it into gear, before ramming on the gas. I jerked back into the seat with a gasp and a laugh.

We raced down the road leaving a plume of dust. I swear, it felt like the powerful engine shook the very fillings in my teeth. My chest vibrated like I was standing next to the bass speaker at a concert. A hysterical laugh tore out of me, making me sound like I was on my first roller coaster.

He screeched to a stop at the T at the end of the street, and turned left, taking us up a hardly used road. Excitement danced through my stomach at each little hill he leaped over.

"Having fun?" he yelled over the engine noise.

"Yes!" I screamed back. The wind twisted my hair, and I felt alive and free.

We leaped over another bump in the hill, bouncing hard.

Both of us yelled. The grass in the field next to us was a yellow blur, and the air smelled crisp and cool.

He slowed at a pull off and turned the beast around.

"This car is amazing," I said.

"She's snappy." We started back toward my house. "So I'm going to the swing dance tonight."

Wait a minute here. I cautiously glanced over at him. Was he about to ask me out? It seemed like our friendship had been building for months in this direction. Was I ready? My gaze dropped to my foot. Could I even dance in this? A vision of a hippo stomping on cowboy boots flashed through my mind.

He shifted and stepped on the gas as we swung out of a turn.

"You should come," he said calmly.

I knew it! "Tonight?"

"Nah. On the weekend. Half the town is going. I'm meeting Maggie Potter there. Do you know her?"

A chill whipped down my spine that had nothing to do with my hair blowing in the wind. My brain stuttered, trying to process what he'd just said. Wait. What? He wasn't asking me, after all. I gulped. "Wow! How long have you known her?" It was a lame attempt to stall for time as I tried to comprehend.

"Oh, off and on for a few years. I've been seeing a lot of her lately since I started working on her car." Was his tone being extra careful right now? Like he was feeling me out and was worried what my reaction was going to be?

I blew out a deep puff of air as I tucked my hair back behind my ear for something to do. I had no right to be too disappointed. After all, I never knew where I wanted to be with him, myself.

"That's great, Richie! You two will have a lot of fun." I pointed to my foot. "I think I'll sit this one out. I'd hate to cause anyone bodily harm with my extreme left foot dance moves."

His shoulders relaxed, and he laughed. His fingers waggled against the steering wheel as if stretching. He must have really been anxious. "You'll do fine. It will be fun. I think you should come."

We were heading back to the T again.

"I'll think about it," I said. He obviously wasn't going to take no for an answer, and I didn't want to argue.

A few minutes later he pulled into my driveway.

I patted the dash affectionately. "She's amazing."

"She really is," Richie agreed.

"Thanks for the ride. I'll see you later, okay? Have fun at the dance!" I opened the door and swung my leg out.

He ducked down to see me below the door frame. "I'm still hoping to see you there!"

I shrugged and slammed the door, before waving. He waved back and then turned to look out the rear window, slowly backing out.

Wow. That was a change of events. I glanced at my watch, kind of grateful to see it was time for me to head down to the realty office. After a quick trip inside to grab my purse and lock the door, I hobbled over to my rental car.

Driving with a walking cast was a whole new experience, even though it was on my left foot. It was clunky and heavy and hot. I sighed, feeling like the weight of the world had suddenly descended on me.

How did I feel about this news that Richie was interested in another woman? I wrinkled my nose. There was that unfamiliar heat prickling inside me, the kind that made me hide my head in a hole. Stinging pride. To be honest, even if I wasn't sure if I was into him, it had made me feel good that he'd liked me. That we'd had a special friendship.

And now I had to share him.

Shows how well I could read men. Another sigh escaped, half twisting into a groan at the end. Some things were not meant to be. People always said it was about the timing. Well, somehow, it was always off for me.

I pulled into Flamingo Realty and parked under the giant pink bird on the sign. As I entered, Uncle Chris was already approaching my desk. He was either a psychic or had heard me pull up.

"How'd you know I was here?" I asked.

Uncle Chris handed me the message. "That foot of yours pounding on the steps. Check out your newest listing.

Contract has been signed and I need you to go over there and get the lock box on."

I accepted the paper and squinted to read the address. Reeter's Ridge. It was in the next town over. "Do you know them? Who is it?"

"The owner is actually deceased. Trustee account is representing. The guy, Mr. Brown, died last month."

"Oh, wow. Okay. Does he have family?" I noticed the house was expensive.

"No one immediate. His estate is to be sold to pay his creditors and the rest will be going to his mother."

"His mother? That's so sad. The poor woman."

"Yeah. She's in a retirement home in Florida."

This was going to be my first time being a selling agent for someone who wasn't actually alive. I frowned as I read the address again. "Have you done this type of thing before? How complicated is it going to be?"

He shrugged his shoulders, his jacket hanging on both sides like elephant ears. I eyed it, realizing he needed to get that fitted.

"Don't worry. It will work out," he reassured me.

"Uncle Chris, are you losing weight?" We'd had a stressful few weeks, and I wondered if it was getting to him.

"Maybe a little. Anyway, the property executive is an old friend of mine. We went to school together eons ago. He had this come across his desk and thought of me. Easy money, right?"

Easy money except it was in the town next door. Not exactly convenient. Still, who was I to turn down money? The last few house sales had helped me dig myself out of the hole, but now I had a ton of medical bills.

I nodded firmly. "Terrific, I'll head over there later today. Anything else?"

"Well, you know Oscar is petitioning the court with the new evidence that the judge has previous prejudices against your mom. It looks like they will be taking that into account at the next parole meeting."

Oscar was my grandfather, someone both Uncle Chris and my father had reconnected with after a twenty-year estrangement. It was odd and at the same time wonderful to hear his name come out of my uncle's mouth.

"Why can't we just get her out now?" I asked. It seemed pretty cut and dried. She was being held for a crime someone else had committed. We finally had the proof.

"It's not as easy as that. You know how the law works... very slowly. To get her out, we'd need to ask for a new trial. The hope is that she will be out on her parole by the time that's tackled. The attorney is confident this will all be expunged from her record, but we want to get her out the fastest way possible." Uncle Chris patted his pocket for his cigar. "We have to take it one step at a time, but things are looking very positive."

I nodded. "I have a visit with her scheduled. I can't wait. I'm hoping Dad's going to come."

"Wow." Uncle Chris exhaled deeply. "That will be big."

"How about you? You ready to see her?"

He glanced down, and I noticed his normally ruddy skin took on a darker hue. "There's a lot there for me to process yet, Stella. I really don't know how I'm going to face her."

My uncle was not an emotional guy. Seeing him look ashamed made me nervous. I'd told him before not to feel guilty, but sometimes words didn't do any good. Sometimes it was a heart issue. I didn't know how to deal with that.

All I could think of to do was to change the subject. "So— uh—the house is vacant?"

"Yep. Ever since Mr. Brown died." His voice was stronger, like he was relieved he was back on solid ground. He managed to get his cigar out. He bit off the tip and spat it in the direction of the trash can.

"How did he die?"

"The official report was that he was a victim of a hunting accident." His forehead furrowed. "For as long as I've lived around here I'd never considered that a hunting area. I'm kind of surprised how they came to that conclusion so fast."

"Yikes! Like you suspect something else happened?"

"I mean, who am I to question the police findings? Still, David Brown was an interesting character. He has quite a history working at a local bank. I'm sure there's more to the story."

"Why do you say that?" I asked.

"He was an odd duck but I'll have to tell you more about

that later. I'm actually running late. I have a meeting in just a bit with the city council."

Uncle Chris had some political ambitions for this little Pennsylvania town. He used to be all talk, but lately, his actions were moving in that direction as well.

He headed out while I wobbled to the store room. I had to get the pink flamingo for-sale sign we were famous for.

I scooped up the plastic bird and then the lock box and was on my way to Gainesville.

The city of Gainesville was quaint, with the original buildings in what they called their Town Square. The blocks were lined with hanging flowers and original light posts. It actually was quite cute.

To the right of me were the Appalachian mountains. Immediately the cute feeling disappeared as my GPS led me in that direction. The mountains rose, dark and foreboding. Apprehension crept like actual fingers down my spine. I tried to swallow and rationalize my emotions. Maybe I was feeling this way because my car accident had taken place on a mountain road.

But it felt like something else. These mountains felt oppressive, like they were hiding secrets. Bad secrets. And it felt like they were warning me that I could be one of them.

I shivered as I turned up the road.

2

The temperature dropped, and the further I drove up, the colder it got. It seeped into the car like an ill omen and curled around my face and hands. I twisted the heater dial and tried to ignore the creepy-crawlies dancing along my spine.

After all, there was nothing to be freaked out about.

Uh, you're selling a dead man's house. A death that Uncle Chris already questioned, my subconscious reminded me. It was always charmingly helpful that way.

I brushed the thought out of my mind and focused on Richie. Richie and his datey date date. I rolled my neck. Now that some time had passed to process the idea, I wasn't as bothered about it as I thought I would be. The worst thing about it was the feeling that someone had moved in on my territory, even if I only considered him a friend. Still, Richie deserved to be happy. He was such a great guy. And I already knew that he was someone who was always going to remain a good friend.

I could live with that. He was awfully sweet.

The road curved under the trees and my tires kicked up piles of fallen leaves. They riffled behind the car like an organic display of 'just married' cans. I was amazed at how isolated it was up here. Apparently the town had spurned this elevation climb for the comforts of the valley below.

Although, after the last winter, I could understand why. This drive would be a bear in the ice and snow.

Mr. Brown. Banker Brown. Uncle Chris called you an odd duck with an interesting story. A hunting accident, huh? Is that what happened to you?

The higher I went, the darker and more overgrown the route became. I swallowed, not so eager to be out here alone in a hunting area myself.

I wondered what Mr. Brown had looked like. With a name like Mr. Brown, my mind immediately pieced together a short, tubby little man with a brown suit and a brown bowler hat.

Nonsense. Modern men don't wear bowler hats. Was there even such a thing anymore? I tried to imagine him with a baseball cap instead. But try as I might, the cartoonish image persisted, complete with a gold pocket watch.

I wondered if he had the gold watch on when he died. Would it have reflected in the sun and prove to the hunter that he wasn't an animal?

I shook my head, amazed at the way my mind conjured up stories.

A new question occurred to me. What would happen to all of Mr. Brown's belongings? How about his furniture, cars, and clothing? Was the house left exactly like it had been the day he died? That was creepy.

I glanced at the paper in the seat next to me and decided to give Mr. Brown's estate trustee a call. There was no one behind me. In fact I hadn't seen a car the entire time on this mountain road.

I slowed down and got the number voice dialed. A moment later, it was abruptly answered, "How can I direct your call?"

"Hi, there. I'm Stella O'Neil, with Flamingo Realty. I'm heading out to deliver a lock box to a house you represent for Mr. Brown."

I was put on hold for a moment before a man picked up. "My name is Mr. Coleman, the trustee for David Brown's Estate. What can I do for you?"

"I was wondering if you had any special requests as I get this place ready to show. Are you including the furniture in the sale?"

"We are."

"Okay, good to know. What about his personal belongings'?"

"We had a cleanup crew go through and pack everything up last week." There was some hesitation. "Because of Mr. Brown's background, there has been some unwanted interest."

Wait. What? "His background? I thought he was a banker."

"He was an auditor with Century Bank."

"So, he counted the money or something?"

"No, he was a security box auditor."

"Really. What does that mean, exactly?"

"When a renter would miss their payment and the box was closed, he would be there with the head clerk as they drilled open the lock. And then he would take inventory of what was in the box before it was shipped to a storing facility."

"I see," I said. I really didn't. What did this have to do with causing curiosity at his house?

"Well, there was a big lawsuit at the last bank where he worked. People were suing because all their items went missing. It amounted to nothing because of the clause the bank has in their contract for safety deposit boxes. But, understandably, people are out for blood, and they blame Mr. Brown and think he may have known where the missing items were."

"Ahhh." Now it made sense.

"Because of that, there might be some unwanted attention during this house sale. Most likely not, but you never know in these cases."

"Looky-loos, maybe," I suggested.

"Exactly."

"Was Mr. Brown ever a suspect or involved in the lawsuit?"

"I believe everyone involved was put under a magnifying glass. No criminal charges were ever filed."

"I see." What I saw was that I needed to do some research into this and STAT. "So, as far as the house goes, it's clean and such?"

"Everything is good to go. If you could please make sure that all the interior doors remain closed to help keep it energy efficient. There is a vacuum in the upstairs closet, but if it needs more attention than that, let us know. We'll have the cleaning service return."

"Got it. And the money from the sale will be going to Mr. Brown's mother?"

"Yes, after your commission and his estate obligations are made, the remainder will be in an account for her care."

"Interesting. This is my first time in a situation like this."

"We do it all the time. Feel free to call us if you have more questions." His voice was confident.

"I will. I'm sure there won't be any problems. Hopefully we will get this sold soon."

"Thank you. It's nice to be working with you."

With that, we both hung up. I needed to pay attention to the road. The elevation had risen even more and fog had settled in.

Mr. Brown was becoming more interesting by the second, I mused as I took the first turn, an unmarked road to the left.

I would have thought I was on the wrong street except for a mail box tucked into the corner. Two of them. I bumped down the dirt road and stopped in front of a driveway.

Odd. There was a for-sale sign already in place. It was from a different realty company, however. I put a call in to Mr. Coleman.

"Hello," he answered, when I was eventually patched through.

"Hi, again. I'm sorry to bother you so soon after our last phone call, but the Landmark realty has put up a sign."

"Oh, you can take that down. We had contacted them before we were referred to your uncle. I'll let them know to come collect the sign."

"Okay, Thank you."

We hung up again.

I still hadn't seen the house, as the driveway took a turn behind a grove of trees and disappeared into the haze. I climbed out of the car. Immediately, the misty air wrapped around me with clammy arms. The trees stood dark and mysterious—threatening even—in their shrouds of fog. After hobbling over, I unhooked the competitor's sign from the pole, pinching one of my fingers in the process, and fastened our own. I sucked my finger as I dropped the sign in the lawn. What a weird experience this was turning into.

Weird didn't come close to describing it.

3

I returned to the car and shut the door with a puff, feeling like I'd just run a marathon with the effort of lugging around my clunky leg.

The driveway led around a small bend, and then the mist parted, and Mr. Brown's house came into view. My mouth dropped. The structure appeared perched on a cliff's edge, like a gray moth clinging to the tip of a branch.

The reality that I was going to have to go inside made my stomach sink. To say I didn't like heights was an understatement. I was one of those people who avoided glass elevators and stayed near the wall on high-rise balconies. So this steel structure definitely had my adrenaline pumping.

Obviously, this meant I could adjust the listing description. One lovely thing about the home was the view of the Appalachian mountain range. "Killer views," I murmured as I climbed out, taking the lock box with me.

Who would want to live like this? Daredevils? Clinging to a mountain's side, just waiting for a strong wind gust to gobble the house up. It gave me the shivers.

The front of the building only had three windows, small inset square windows that gave the building a formidable blocky appearance. I assumed there were more windows on the other side, but from this point of view the place almost resembled a prison.

Mr. Brown, Mr. Brown. Why had you hidden yourself away like this?

The wind whistled through the gutter overhead with a low moan. I swear it sounded like a human voice. It felt like David Brown was trying to answer my question, and by the sound of the moan, it wasn't an answer I was going to like.

I shivered and turned around, trying to take in my surroundings. Where exactly had the owner died by a hunter's stray bullet? On the road?

The wind ripped through my sweater. I rubbed my arms as I limped up the path to the door, on the way spotting a piece of trash winking in the pale sunlight. It was a pop can and full of cigarette ash. I assumed it was cigarette, anyway. I picked it up with the expectation of finding a trashcan inside and continued to the cement landing.

As I took the first step, something hit me hard on the top of my head. I screamed and ducked under my arm, sending the pop can flying. My fat boot caught on the edge of the step, and I stumbled backwards. Luckily, I caught the wrought-iron railing in a death grip and saved myself from falling.

A rock bounced on the ground next to me. And then another. Covering my head, I hurried up the rest of the steps for the safety of the porch roof.

What was this place? I stared up at the sky in horror. Where on earth were the stones falling from?

A caw screeched through the cold autumn air, making the hair on my neck prickle with fear. There was a bird right above me. Carefully, I leaned out and peered up at the porch roof.

Perched on the gutter, a black crow tipped his head and stared me straight in the eye. He hopped along the gutter. His claws scraped against the metal edge.

A raspy sound made me turn to the left. Two birds? This one croaked even lower than the first. His black eye glittered before he cawed again.

I swallowed, remembering how my English professor denounced crows and ravens as carriers of ill-luck.

The speakers asks the raven to tell him its name and it says it will not. Edgar Allan Poe's 1846 essay, "The Philosophy of Composition."

I tried to shrug it off. I was not going to let my imagination get to me, not this time. My gaze dropped to the rock on the step. Had they purposely dropped rocks on me? Why?

I stared out at the car, trying to envision how the return trip to it would look like.

Never mind. I'll think about that later.

I pulled the key from my pocket and faced the door. Not even one step inside and already this place was bad news. I jammed the key in and tried to turn. Great. The door lock was sticky. I twisted and turned, and eventually had it unlocked. I hid the key inside the programed lock box and then clicked the box around the door handle. Grabbing the handle with a deep breath of air, I entered.

The interior greeted me with a dark hush. I shut the door behind me. I winced. The click sounded extra loud. A scent wrapped around me, lemony, like furniture polish. But there was something else. Something stale. Weird.

All the doors were shut, per the trustee's instructions. But, oddly, it seemed that the window blinds had been closed as well. Did we really need the blackout curtains pulled down to the sill? It certainly didn't make for a welcoming experience.

I limped across the room to where huge cathedral windows took up one wall. I reached for the cord and yanked. The curtains shivered for a moment and then parted to reveal the view.

I gasped. The fog was lifting. Beyond the deck was a drop

off to a deep valley with low blue mountains traipsing along the horizon.

I unlocked the sliding glass door and stepped out onto the porch, my booted foot making muffled thumps. I was too scared to go over to the railing, and stopped in the middle of the deck. *I can't do it,* my guts screamed. *You are safe,* another part of me countered.

My body wouldn't quit screaming danger, and my legs felt weak from the height, so I hummed a crazy commercial jingle I'd just heard on the radio. Anything to distract myself.

The yard rolled away from the foot of the house down a slope, like a gentleman giving a low bow at the end of a play.

I took in the forest that I could see. Movement caught my eye. I gasped at the sight of two deer at the bottom of the property.

One stared up, alerted by my noise. His clear dark eyes watched. Then, with a flick of his ear, he went back to grazing.

How interesting he wasn't scared of me. It was weird they were around at all, given how Mr. Brown had died in some weird hunting accident.

The sudden thought of Mr. Brown being shot made me feel exposed out here on the deck. I shivered and hurried indoors, not wanting to be a statistic myself.

Back inside, I was happy to see the kitchen had beautiful white cupboards and was squeaky clean. The smooth gray quartz counter top reflected rectangles of light from the windows. I couldn't resist running my fingers against its silky coolness.

Sitting in the center was a glass vase filled with billowing flowers. I reached for a velvety leaf of one of the flowers and frowned at the touch. Lovely as they were, they were fake.

Their fakeness jarred me and made me realize that something was off about the house. I held my breath to listen.

It was too quiet. Eerie.

In every house I'd shown before there was always some sign of life, a clock ticking, the refrigerator humming. Even a lawn mower or a neighbor's barking dog.

But this house.... It felt dead.

Like its owner.

Nice one, Stella. Typical that I'd geared myself up with some morbid thoughts just in time to explore the rest of the place. I rolled my shoulders and then hobbled boldly down the hallway, going from dusk to dark with all the doors shut.

I opened the first door and peered into the room. A guest bedroom. Along one wall were windows with their curtains pulled tightly shut like the eyelids of a sleeping giant.

The next room was the exact replica of the first. There was a bed and a dresser, and I knew from the trustee that all of this furniture was to be included with the house. Remembering his rule, I shut the door behind me.

My phone rang, making me jump. I fumbled to get it out, amazed at how tightly wound-up I was.

"Stella, you still there?" Uncle Chris's voice boomed. His voice made me cringe, sounding extraordinarily loud in this quiet cave of a house.

"Yeah, just checking everything out." I found myself whispering.

"Good. You finding everything okay?"

"Yes. It's a strange place though."

"Strange how?"

I frowned, not at all sure how to explain it to him. Getting pelted with rocks by birds? Wind wailing in human words? Deer happily grazing in what was supposed to be a hunting area?

"I guess I'm just curious where the owner died. Do you know?"

"I'll have to look that up. Why? You feeling his ghost?"

I shivered at the word and hit the light switch. Groaning, I looked up. Nothing appeared from the bucket light nearly fifteen feet up. That bulb was going to be great fun to replace.

"Why were you calling again?" I asked.

"Sorry, girl. I didn't mean to tease you. You're okay. I've sold lots of houses through trustees. This isn't the first time an accident happened."

"Unless it wasn't an accident," I mumbled.

"Well, there's nothing you can do about that, now. Anyway, I called to tell you that you have a client on his way. He should be there within the hour."

An hour in this place. Lovely. I wanted to complain, but

didn't want Uncle Chris to think I couldn't hack it. "Okay, sounds good." I said, and he signed off.

I shoved the phone away and stared down the hallway. Still one more door to open. I continued down the hall, expecting another bedroom. Opening it revealed another shock. It was a staircase, black as the night. A cold gust rolled out of it, making me wonder if there was a window opened down there. I exhaled deeply, carefully gripped the rail, and started down.

The steps were carpeted, which surprisingly most buyers complained about. I mentally prepared my rebuttal statement about how it could be pulled up and recovered with a laminate of your choice.

The handrail was a twisted black iron, peculiar, old-fashioned, yet an elegant touch. Each step increased the strange damp sensation that seemed to rise from the hidden depths to meet me. I squinted to see the area below. It was much darker down here than above.

Finally, I reached the bottom and stepped into a large family room of some type. Instead of a TV, the central focal point of the room was a huge desk.

There was a door to the right. I took a quick peek inside to see a spare room with a metal folding chair in the corner. It struck me as unusual because there were no windows. Frowning, I shut the door. I'd have to think of how to word that in the listing. It couldn't be a bedroom without a window. I turned my attention back to the desk.

It was an executive desk, and it was in shambles with the drawers half pulled out and items scattered across the top. Everything else in this place was as neat as a pin. Why had the cleaners left this in such a mess? Had someone else rummaged through it since then?

It was too dark in here. I flipped on a light and pushed back the curtains, then returned to the desk.

The desk was beefy with solid legs and a top. Had it come from one of the banks? It must weigh a good two hundred pounds. Who knows how they got it down those stairs but I imagine it came with a lot of back-popping moments.

Yet as clumsy as it looked, there were certain nuances about it that made it appealing, especially how the light danced off of the grain that seemed to glow with the honey swirls.

Curious, I reached for one of the papers that rested on the top and flipped it over. It was an old receipt from the local grocery store. Five pounds of rice, three cans of coffee. Strange.

Underneath that was a leather-bound notebook. I flipped through the pages.

Oddly, the first few sheets had been cut out, leaving the rest blank. I placed it back and opened the top drawer the rest of the way. It was empty, with the exception of a rolling pen and a purse-sized package of tissue. I was about to close it when something else caught my attention.

The depth seemed wrong for such a wide drawer. I removed the pen and tissues and then felt along the bottom.

The wood sprang eagerly from under my fingertips. I ran my fingernail around the edge to see if there was a catch and found a tiny divot in the wood. I pressed it and grinned as the wood bottom bounced up.

With a feeling that I was being naughty, I lifted it up and peeked under the bottom.

My eyes locked onto a key.

WOW! I bet I looked like the Cheshire Cat as I picked it up to examine it. But a second later, the smile wiped off my face. It wasn't some cool skeleton key. It was modern and could have gone to a million things. In fact, I probably had three similar-appearing ones on my own keyring.

After glancing around for any conspicuous key hole, I dropped the key and pressed back the false bottom. I chucked in the tissues and pen and shut the drawer.

It was then that I noticed the drawer below it stuck out a tiny bit as well. I started to reach for it.

"Hello!" A woman called.

I jerked my hand back, my heart racing like a hamster on a wheel. With a guilty flush, I realized the buyer must have arrived.

I hobbled over to the bottom of the stairs, calling. "Hello? I'll be right there."

Just as I started up the stairwell, a tiny part of me reminded me that I'd better be careful. I was isolated, and a quick glance around made me realize there was no way out down here. I was trapped.

"I'm Mrs. Taylor!" the voice called. "I live next door!"

The neighbor! I took the stairs as fast as my foot would allow me.

As I rounded the corner to the entry way, I froze.

Standing in the doorway was my mother.

4

L ight from the open doorway highlighted the tiny figure. I blinked hard.

"Well, hi there! Nice to see someone finally in this place," a sweet voice said as the woman walked inside.

Wait a minute, what was I thinking? Talk about a brain trick—I must be losing my mind. Or this place was making me crazy. This woman had the same slight figure and hair style as my mom, but Mom was still in the Ashmount prison awaiting her parole trial. Sure, life had been pretty strange and unexpected lately, but what I just experienced was almost a hallucination. Was there something wrong with me? Should I go to the doctor? Was it some frantic longing to finally have her home that had caused this?

It was then I noticed a little limp. It drew my attention like a stop sign, probably because of my own gimpy leg. She smiled, and her eyes lit up. Instantly I liked her. It wasn't often you met someone whose smile touched their eyes. In fact the people I usually ran into wore guarded polite masks and acted like smiles cost money.

"Hi, there," I said, walking over with my hand out. I have to be honest. I was still a little freaked out over the weird vision I'd just had. "I'm Stella, the realtor for this place."

"Oh, nice to meet you. Isn't it a beautiful day?" Her voice warbled high, and she brushed her hand in the air rather than reaching for mine. That caught me off guard as I wondered what she was doing until I saw a fly buzzing around her head. "Darn fly. They're always after me because I'm so sweet." She held out her hand. "I'm Charlotte Taylor. Like I said, I'm the neighbor."

She glanced down at my foot. "What happened, ducky?"

"Car accident. It's nearly healed. The doctor just wants me to wear it for another week. I feel like I've been in it forever."

"Well, it's good it's getting better. Keep an eye on it. At least you're not like me. My leg is a good three inches shorter than the other. And I need every inch I can get! Being only five feet tall. My grandma always used to call me short stack, but she was shorter than me. Anyway, I wear this shoe with a tall heel, but it's still funny. It's my special leg," she finished with a grin.

She was a hoot.

We shook hands, and she continued in her high rushed

words, "I hope you don't mind me popping in. I couldn't help it after seeing that fancy flamingo sign!"

"Of course not!" I answered.

She glanced around the foyer. "It's such a shame about what happened to that poor man, but I'm so happy to know the place won't be sitting here vacant."

"I agree. We will have the right neighbors in here in no time. I'm sure it was all such a shock."

"Oh, you have no idea. Such a shock. There I was out on my sundeck with my ebook reader when the gunfire went off. Twice!" Charlotte shivered. "Those sounds are terrifying. They sound like death."

Wow! Practically an eye witness. "That must have been terrifying. Are there hunters in here very often? I saw the deer."

"I've never had anything like that happen in the entire time that I've lived here. Of course, I've only been here a short while. But it's been very quiet and private. Honestly, you'd think the police would have jumped into more action. After all, there are houses down on the other side of those trees. You can't see them, but they're there. I'm not sure how the hunters even thought they had the space to do that here."

We walked out onto the front porch. "How well did you know Mr. Brown?"

She flushed. "This makes me sound so unneighborly, but I didn't know him at all. He was kind of mysterious. Can you believe the entire time I've lived here, I never even saw him.

He's a recluse. I didn't even see him when his groceries would get dropped off. They'd bring the bags up to his door, and then...." She waved her fingers vaguely, making it seem like the food magically disappeared.

The wind stirred dust from the road into a miniature tornado. It whisked through the dying flower garden and the remaining standing stalks rasped like skeleton fingers.

Just then, another rock fell from overhead and rattled down the steps.

Charlotte glanced up and clucked her tongue. "Those darn birds. They just popped up out of nowhere. They've been something awful recently. Harbingers of death, my grandpa used to say. Brandon from the grocery store, told me they have video footage of some guy throwing rocks at them in the parking lot. Those birds dive bombed the man until he ran to his car and I guess they decorated the windshield in their own special way. Serves him right! Not animals you want to mess with."

"I hope they're not mad that I'm selling this house," I answered, a little worried. Harbingers of death? Why were they here?

Her eyebrows raised in interest, and I thought she had a question for me, but then her phone rang. She tugged it from her pocket and glanced at it. Her nose wrinkled.

"I'm so sorry, but I have to take this. So nice to meet you," she said, with an absentminded wave. Turning quickly in the direction of her house, she jabbered into her phone before I had time to lift my hand and say goodbye.

I watched her leave, thinking about what a fun character she was. And Mr. Brown never met her. How odd was that?

Overhead, the crow cawed again. *Go away, Mr. Harbinger!* What was I going to do about those birds? Put a sign up to warn all potential buyers to watch for falling rocks? That'd go over well.

I checked my watch. The client Uncle Chris called me about was supposed to arrive any minute. To kill time, I yanked the dead flower stalks out of the pot and carried them to the side of the house to toss them.

Was this the way Mr. Brown had gone that fateful day? Charlotte hadn't finished her story after she said she'd heard the gun shots. Did that mean she found him? Or had she shrugged the sounds off as fireworks or something and never investigated?

I walked along the side of the house until I could see the sloping land behind it. The sun felt weird. Not sure how to explain it. Bright, but in a tinny way, making all the colors feel washed out in an underlying haze.

I heard the car approach and walked back toward to the front. Just before I rounded the corner, I saw something in the trim. A weird nick, with raw wood exposed.

The car pulled into the driveway and let out a horn blast. I hastened around the corner to see an old battered car with a dented fender and cracked windshield.

The engine shut off with a few ticks, and a man climbed out. He was heavy-set, wearing a thick-framed pair of glasses, jeans and a dirty t-shirt, and very worn sneakers. A load of fast food wrappers, water bottles, and papers fell out of the car with the opened door. He scooped them up and chucked everything back in, then wiped his hand on his already greasy hair. Instantly, I was curious what he was doing here. This did not seem like the type of house that would interest him at all.

"Hi, there. I'm Stella O'Neil, from Flamingo Realty," I said, infusing my voice with confidence. I did not want to offer my hand.

"Well, aren't you cute? Name's Gary Studebaker." he said with a fleshy grin. I noticed he had a cigarette tucked behind his ear. His second chin hung like a gunny sack and wobbled with his smile. "Hurt your leg, hmm?" His grin grew bigger as he pushed up his glasses and most obviously stared at my legs.

I straightened and crossed my arms, instantly on guard. My booted foot seemed to scream weakness. "It's fine. All right. Are you ready? The house is already unlocked."

I checked for the birds as I headed up the stairs, but they seemed to have disappeared. I opened the door and waved my hand so that he could enter first.

He hung back, apparently waiting for me.

"Please. I insist. I'll follow you," I said firmly. There was no way I was going to allow Mr. Leerer to walk behind me.

He grinned, showing more teeth than I cared to see, and sauntered across the threshold.

I followed, doing an odd thing. I left the front door open. My gut warned me to keep a sharp eye out and I always trusted my gut.

We entered the living room, looking much brighter and welcoming than when I'd first arrived. Of course, he stopped in front of the windows just as I'd expected him to do. The view was a show-stopper.

With his hands clasped behind him, he rocked on his heels. "So, I hear this house was custom built for the owner, is that right?"

I was a little surprised to hear him say that. Those types of details are normally found in the listing description, and I'd noticed Mr. Brown's trustee had avoided mentioning that. I could understand why. It seemed that nowadays people wanted a blank slate, not something that had already been designed for someone else.

"Yes, that's right. But, of course, you can put your own unique taste to it."

"Hm, taste," he said with a sly grin.

I was not liking this. Not one bit.

"So, what's down there?" Gary pointed to the hallway, and gave his glasses a nudge up the bridge of his nose again.

"The bedrooms and the study. The entire upper floor is dedicated to the living space."

"Well, I suppose I should go look at it, hmm?"

"Absolutely. Like I said, you'll see that the rooms are blank canvasses. Ready for someone to put their stamp on it."

He glanced inside the first room before pursing his lips. "Where's the master bedroom?"

I pointed down the hall to the master.

He grinned, seeming to notice how far I stood behind him. "Come on in. Show me around."

I swallowed hard. "Absolutely." My hand dove into my jacket pocket where I kept my keys. As I smiled, I slid a key between my fingers. If he tried any funny business, I was prepared to claw his face out.

We walked into the bedroom and he slowly spun around. His eyes were fast, glancing in the corners. Swiftly, he walked the perimeter of the room, studying the baseboards.

This guy was getting odder by the minute.

"He slept in here?" he asked, his eyebrows bunching up. He pulled out a drawer and looked inside. It was empty, but it still made me feel icky.

"I'm assuming so," I said.

"This doesn't look like a man's room," he noted.

I got it. The movers had come through and removed the personal effects of the man, leaving a gray bedspread, and two dressers. There was very little left to show anyone had lived here at all.

"The house has been stripped so they could do a generic staging," I explained.

He gave a cheesy grin at my careless word and I grimaced.

"Stripped, huh?"

"Of his personal items. Everything left comes with the house."

He nodded. We walked back to the hallway, and he yanked opened the last door to the stairs. "And down there?"

"A family room area, a bathroom, and a bonus room," I said, hoping there were no nasty surprises. I hadn't actually fully explored the bottom floor before Charlotte had interrupted me.

We headed down the stairs with me, once again, encouraging him to lead. At the bottom, he immediately walked through the open doorway to the right.

Wait a minute. How was the bonus room's door open? I was positive I'd shut it when I came through earlier. It must have a tricky latch that I needed to watch.

"Not much in here," he noted as he walked inside. He moved the chair to look behind it. His nose wrinkled when he found nothing. Turning around, he grunted in surprise as he noted the same thing I had when I first entered. "No windows."

"I'm not sure how this room was used. Maybe as a music room or study? You could get a contractor out here to see if it's possible to add a window. I don't see why it wouldn't be."

Appearing dissatisfied, he wandered back to the family

room. I shut the door behind us and gave the handle a wiggle.

"Why are you frowning?" Gary asked, surprising me. I hadn't realized he hadn't continued into the family room.

"Was I? It's nothing." I gave him my super confident grin but still felt confused about the open door. The latch hadn't felt tricky.

He raised an eyebrow as if trying to figure me out, and then walked over to the desk. "Messy! This come with the house, too?"

"Yes, it does. It's an exceptional piece, isn't it?"

He pulled out a few drawers and hummed at discovering they were empty.

"Would you like to head back up and check out the upstairs deck?" I asked.

"Yeah. Let's do it."

Gripping my keys firmly, I led him upstairs to the living room. It had been way too dark down there, and it was a relief to be back upstairs, bright from the giant windows.

I yanked open the sliding glass door. Even I had to admit the landscape was amazing. The sky was finally clear, a slice of blue above the mountains, while the autumn breeze carried scents of fallen leaves and sap. "Like you saw when you first came in, this is our show stopper."

He walked out onto the deck, giving an impressed whistle. "You really can't beat this scenery, can you?"

"I'd say it's a million dollar view."

"It would be, if that house wasn't right next door." He pointed.

I nodded. It was odd that Charlotte's house was so close, and it did distract from the feeling of isolated wilderness.

We headed back inside, and I handed him my card. He said he'd be in touch and gave me a wink.

I watched him drive away with a sigh of relief and a relaxing of my tense shoulders. Pulling out my own car keys, I stared at them for a second, realizing I needed to get myself a better self-defense weapon.

I locked the front door and, carefully, gripped the handrail and hobbled down. Above me, a raspy caw ripped through the air. I covered my head out of instinct and dashed to the car. After jumping in, I saw the crow was watching me from the gutter, his head tipped.

Then he let out another screech, wings stretched out and flapped away. I swear he was warning me.

And without good intent.

5

I rested my head against the seat and watched the crow fly away. It was then I noticed something on my shoulder. I jumped and nearly screamed before I realized it was a tiny black feather. It quivered in the air of my exhale. I plucked it off and flicked it out the window.

Was it possible that our real estate could be sued from some client getting beaned in the head with a rock? I needed to talk to someone about what to do about the birds. I'd heard of people using scarecrows. Would something like that work? I shook my head glumly. If I couldn't scare them, I doubted any straw man could.

There had to be some answer.

I grabbed my phone to see if Uncle Chris had any ideas and saw an old text from Carlson. It was nothing really, just a joke about how he'd had to miss his dinner while pulling over a food truck. He was a police officer with the Brookfield department, and I'd had more than a few run-ins with him. He was kind of a grumpy guy but some of that grumpiness seemed to fit me. We'd actually become good friends, as unlikely of a duo as that created.

Aww, Carlson. Seeing his text, I realized how much I missed him. Like really missed him. I hadn't seen him in weeks. Maybe I could talk him into getting a late lunch now. I figured I'd give it a shot and texted, —**You still hungry?**

I smiled as I read it, hoping the answer was yes.

He did not disappoint. —**Yeah. Just got off my shift. Want to meet at the diner?**

I knew which diner he meant, the one and only Springfield with its legendary burgers. After glancing at the time I typed, —**I can be there in thirty minutes**

He sent back a thumbs up.

Grinning, I started the car without another glance at the house. I was ready to get out of Dodge and back into town.

The Springfield Diner, with its bright red awnings, was packed like it always was, especially at this time of day. I parked down the street, not even trying to find a spot closer. As soon as I stepped out of the vehicle, the scent of fried onions pulled me closer like an invisible fishing line. The breeze combed through the leaves of the last surviving geraniums inside the diner window's flower boxes.

I walked inside the restaurant and was instantly met with

a pang of disappointment. Marla Springfield, the owner and my friend, was uncharacteristically nowhere in sight.

I felt even worse when I saw the waitress, heading toward me. Her name was Tamra, and she hated me even though I had no idea why. I'd tried everything to win her over, and all I got was a bunch of sneers and subtle insults for my efforts. Even worse, I could never think of a comeback for the insults until the middle of the night.

It was no different now. Tamra curled her lip and asked me if I was sure that I was there to meet a friend. She made me feel like the last kid to get picked at a dodgeball game.

"Yeah, I'm sure. He's right over there." I pointed.

She rolled her eyes and led me over to the table.

Carlson loomed over the table a full head taller than the surrounding patrons. His shaved-bald scalp gleamed in the overhead lights.

He raised his head from the menu as I eased into the booth. "How are you?"

He didn't exactly grin, but I saw the corner of his lip slightly quirk. I swear that man fought any display of happiness.

"Good," I said, then looked for Tamra. Too late, I realized she left before giving me a menu or taking my drink order.

He leaned against the back of the booth, making the wood squeak. "How's the leg? You feeling better?"

"Yeah. Only a few days more and I can get rid of this albatross."

"Albatross. Nice. I bet you can't wait."

I nodded. "Like it's graduation day, baby."

Tamra reappeared with a glass of water for me. She set it down with just enough of a clank to appear careless and chomped her gum. "Your usual?" she asked me, refusing to make eye contact.

Heat crept up into my cheeks that it was common knowledge I ate here so often I had a usual.

"Yeah," I mumbled. Still, who could blame me? Their bacon cheeseburger was to die for.

She took Carlson's order and grabbed his menu before marching off.

"So, what are you doing later on?" Carlson continued after she left. He stretched with his fingers locked behind his neck. A neck that was as thick as a telephone book.

"Well, I just got done with a new house showing, so, unless he calls with an offer, I'll be having a quiet night." Then I studied him. His eyes crinkled with humor. Holy cow. Was he hinting about getting together? "Why? Do you want to go do something?"

Immediately, he straightened forward. "Oh," he said. It was a decidedly weird Oh.

"Oh?" I asked, feeling that cold sweat of discomfort. My encased foot gave a prickly itch in commiseration.

He started again, "Well, I mean, yeah, that sounds fun. But, actually, I have plans." His gaze cut out the window.

Why wasn't he meeting my eyes? "That's cool. You working?"

"No, not that. I, uh, I have a date." He blushed, a ruddiness that filled his ears and crawled down below the collar of his shirt.

A... date? My mouth felt like a dryer lint ball.

"Oh," I said. I guess now it was my turn to sound idiotic. Quickly, I tried to recover. "Who is she? Anyone I know?" I pulled my mouth into a grin, certain I looked somewhere between a clown and a mannequin. *Floor, please for the love of all that's good, open up and swallow me now.*

He shook his head and snorted. "Probably not. I met her on that Ematch site. Kind of crazy, huh?" Now he met my eyes, and it was apparent that since he'd let the cat out of the bag, he decided to let loose his enthusiasm. "So, what do you think?"

What did I think? I think the world felt like it had just shifted sharply on its axis. What the heck was going on around here? Seriously, the same exact thing happening twice to me so close together? Was it some kind of dating epidemic that had apparently decided to skip right over me? Unlike the chicken pox which I swear I had twice while growing up. *You're unworthy of a date.* Frantically, I gulped my water.

"Terrific," I said after finally wiping my mouth. I only hoped the sharp wincing sensation I felt in my gut wasn't showing on my face. This news stung, I had to admit it.

"Yeah, it will be great. So, uh, what's new in your life?" He was so chill, so unobservant to my blatant fire-to-my-soul suffering.

My life? Oh it's about as interesting as watching paint dry. Desperately, I tried to come up with something of interest. *Let's see, I nearly got tagged in the head with a rock from a deranged crow. Oh thank heavens, here comes that burger.*

Tamra set it before me with another clunk and I immediately dug in. Mouth full, can't talk.

"Wow," Carlson was impressed. "You hungry or what?"

"Mmm hmm," I said, shoving a French fry in for good measure. I chewed while he gave his own plate a once over and then reached for the ketchup.

We spent several moments eating before he said, "So what's this about a new house. Lots of interest in it?"

I shrugged. "This one is weird because the seller is actually deceased and a trustee is selling it. All the money is going to a relative."

"Yeah? What house?"

"It's over in Gainesville. But it's kind of cool the house perches on the edge of an overlook of the Appalachian mountain range. There are two of them, actually, built by the same guy."

His eyebrows quirked together. "What's his name? The owner."

"David Brown."

At that he smiled, appearing a little maniacal, to be

honest. I was digesting the thought that his smiles were so rare when he continued, "Ahh, the elusive Mr. Brown."

"You know him?" I asked, surprised.

"Know him?" He snorted like I'd just asked if the Easter Bunny was real. "He was only a part of the biggest scandal that Century Bank has ever been embroiled in. The security boxes? Millions of dollars of items just disappeared."

"I don't know a lot about it. I've been meaning to look into it."

"There's not a lot to learn. Nothing was ever found. Although it's pretty odd that he quit his job soon after and was never seen again. Interesting don't you think?"

"I'd heard he was a recluse."

Carlson shrugged. "There was a welfare check made on him because his withdrawal was so abrupt. He said he was fine, so we had to drop it. Although I would have liked to have had a little one-on-one conversation with the man."

"Why?"

He violently stabbed a French fry into the ketchup. "My grandfather was one of the guys that got fleeced."

"Wow! Are you serious? Your poor grandfather!"

"Yeah. Grandpop lost a bunch of his war memorabilia as well as some old stocks."

"I'm so sorry."

Carlson rubbed his hand across his scalp. "Now you know why some people don't trust banks. The moral of the story—don't keep things in a safety deposit box that you actually want to keep safe."

"Is your grandfather okay now?"

"He's dealt with it. Life's short, you have to move on, right?"

"Yeah." I twirled my straw in the water. "So, I'm guessing you think that Mr. Brown sold the stuff, and that's how he lived?"

"I really don't know. As far as every investigation went, his hands were clean. Not to mention, we haven't uncovered any of the stolen stuff. I mean not even so much as a single coin has showed up in an auction. And trust me, we've had our ear to the ground." He wiped his mouth and took one last drink of his soda.

"Weird." I eyed his empty plate. "Are you going to get dessert?"

He rubbed his hands on the napkin and checked his watch. "Do you mind if I pass? I have things to do and—"

His date. "Oh, yeah. Sure. Uh—have a good time tonight!" I said, as cheery as possible.

He fished around his back pocket for his wallet and pulled out a couple bills. "See you around, Hollywood." He grinned as he slid them under the plate.

I weakly smiled back. Inside, I wanted to drown my humiliation and pain with an enormous chocolate ice-cream sundae. With a side of doughnuts, hold the sprinkles, because—moderation.

As he sauntered toward the door, I tried to appear like a supportive friend and not like a piece of toilet paper dragged off a shoe. What was I even thinking? That Carlson was interested in me? He had never even intended to ask me out.

It seemed right then that everyone around me was suddenly laughing harder, smiling more, and were all infinitely more popular than I'd ever be.

Right then, Tamra sauntered over, this time staring at me like I was a ginormous plate of loser. I smiled, determined to tried to strike up a friendly conversation. "So, how's your day going?"

"Apparently better than yours," she said, eyeing my cast. "Might as well just wear a sign that says you're clumsy."

I tried to laugh it off. "Yeah, not too much longer."

"Ready for your ticket?"

I glumly nodded, and she produced it from a lightly stained apron pocket. I passed my debit card over to her. She grabbed it like I was handing her a dead rat and carried it away.

When she returned, I decided to try and squash this weirdness between us. I took a deep breath, "Tamra, I feel like somehow we got off on the wrong foot. I'm not sure what I did, but have I offended you somehow?"

Her mouth twisted into a frown. "Why would you say that?"

"It seems like you're irritated with me when I come in."

Her mouth opened and then shut firmly. At first, I didn't

think she was going to respond. Then she blurted, "I'm just sick of new people like you just sweeping in here selling off our property. It really irks me. You don't know anything about our town, you don't care. It's just a commodity to you. Especially your new listing up on the mountain." She nodded at my shocked look. "Yeah, I've heard about it. We talk in this town. I bet you don't even know who built it. Or care."

"I—I do care," I sputtered in my defense.

"Whatever. You have a good day, you hear. Watch out for any more falls." She stared coldly at me before marching off, leaving me to gape after her like a baby bird abandoned by its mom.

After Tamra stormed off, I skulked from the restaurant, ducking my head, not wanting to meet anyone's eyes in case they saw the skirmish between the two of us. What if they believed her? Thought I was some uncaring person?

I was relieved to get into the safety of my car, ready to go home and yank the blankets over my head. Wait. What was I saying? This wasn't even my car. It was a rental. I didn't have a car anymore.

Funny how you can feel like the brightest star in the sky one minute, and the next be burning out in the atmosphere as you crash to the ground.

Okay, pull it together, Stella. This is a case of extreme overreaction. What is my real problem here? I thought for a second.

Carlson.

Wow. His news really shook me to my core. I poked through the ashes of my feelings trying to figure out what was going on.

It was obvious to see. I was crushed. Really crushed, actually. Carlson dating hit me in a completely different way than Richie dating. Maybe I'd friend-zoned Richie all along and never realized it until this morning. I rubbed my forehead. Nothing I can do about either one of them now. I knew there had to be someone out there for me. A lid for every pot, right?

What if my pot was so banged up and rusty there wouldn't be a lid that fit?

Wow, this line of thought was getting me nowhere in a hurry. With a deep breath, I tried to regroup. I'll think about all of this later. I'll be okay. I always am. I grabbed my phone and flipped through to my messages.

There was one from Clarence Brighton, Mom's attorney.

"Good news. The parole board received your letter. I was able to talk to the sheriff in the county. They are going to a grand jury to get an indictment against Derek Armstrong, and they will be going after him within the next few days. That plays a big part for your mom's parole hearing. As far as everything I'm hearing, her early release is a go."

Thank you, God. That was the best news ever. I grinned, feeling my heart lifting from the doom and gloom of just moments ago.

Feeling perked up a bit, I dragged out Tamra's condemning statement to examine it. That was pretty intense that she knew about the house, not to mention I was the one representing it. What kind of gossip chain did this town have, anyway?

I needed to figure out what was so amazing about the house that Tamra could accuse me of not caring. Obviously I was missing something, at least according to her.

I decided to call my friend, Kari. Her husband was a land developer, and I figured if anyone knew, he would.

It only rang three times before she picked up.

"Hey Kari, you busy?" I could tell she was by her breathless hello.

"Yeah. I'm on my way to a PTA meeting."

"Do you have time for a quick question?"

"Yes, of course. What's up?"

"Well, I had this weird conversation with a waitress. You know the one at the diner that doesn't like me? She basically accused me of not knowing the history of a house I'm representing. It's kind of true, so I wanted to check if your husband knew anything about the houses up on Reeter's Ridge? Is there anything significant about them that's well known?"

"No, I've never even heard of them."

I immediately felt better. See, Tamra! It's not just me.

She continued, "I'll run it by Joe real quick. Reeter's Ridge, you said?"

"Yep."

"Okay, I'll text you later with what he says."

"Perfect," I said.

"By the way," her voice dropped into a charming tone. "Since I have you on the phone, I need to have you over for dinner soon."

That was a loaded statement. I gulped hard. The last few times she'd invited me to dinner, she had a blind date waiting in the outskirts. It was always some "great family friend whom I know you'll love." I'd yet to find that sentiment true.

I hedged, not wanting to be rude, "Are you feeling up to that? How's the morning sickness?"

"I'm feeling alright. Come on, it'd be fun! I haven't had a chance to hang out with anyone for a long time. I miss my friends!"

Well, no mention of a blind date. Maybe this time would be different. Feeling heartened, I agreed, and we hung up.

Hey, see! I have people who like me. Who cares about Carlson? And when was the last time I'd hung out with anyone? Just like Kari, it had been a while, and I didn't have a pregnancy to blame.

Jumping off of that thought, I texted my friend, Georgie.

—**Hey lady. What's going on? I'm starting to get cabin fever and need to get out.**

Maybe the three of us could do a girl's night. There was that movie I'd been dying to—.

The phone rang, cutting off my thoughts.

"Hello?" I answered.

It was Georgie. "Hi! Sorry for calling but I absolutely detest texting. Not only does spell check hate me, but I also can't type worth beans. How funny that you asked. I was just thinking about you and how we needed to do something soon."

"Great minds! I was thinking we could grab Kari and go see that chick flick this weekend."

"Aww, I can't." She paused for a second, while I digested my third rejection. "I have an idea. Why don't you hang out with a few of us instead? Saturday, we're going to the Barn Hop. Sound fun?"

A few of us? What exactly did that mean? Was it a few friends, or was I going to be a third wheel with her and her boyfriend. "Maybe. Define us."

"Us? Oh, me mostly. Frank might join later. Maybe Kari, too. It's kind of low-key, but there's live music and dancing."

Dancing. I knew what this was now, and who would be there. Richie and his date. I chewed my bottom lip, wondering how I was going to get out of it. "My leg's still kind of gimpy, so I'm definitely not dancing."

"Oh. Right. I still think you should come. There's games and live music. Beer. Good food. I think there's even an ax throwing competition. I'm sure you could do that. Come on. It will be fun."

Her confidence in my ax wielding skills was heart

warming. I grinned. "All right, I'll come, if only to live up to your expectations in my sweet ax skills."

She laughed. My phone vibrated with a text back from Kari, so I said goodbye, and then quickly scrolled to read it.

Kari wrote, —**Joe says it was a construction company named RandCo. They came from out of town to do the job.**

The developer's name sounded as interesting as cold oatmeal. I answered, —**Thank you,** and then typed in RandCo in the search bar to see what I could find.

An ad for the company popped up, with a construction hat and red letters that proclaimed, "Specializing in unique house designs."

How peculiar. Those two houses were nice but not exactly what I'd consider to be unique. It must have been for a special design to overhang the cliff.

But what did this have to do with Tamra, the waitress at the diner? And did this have something to do with the stolen safety deposit boxes?

I searched up the case of the disappearing safety deposit boxes to see if there was any more information on it. I didn't see anything for Century Bank, but I found another story that was strikingly similar with another bank, one called Leafbrook. I scanned the article. Again, it had been old stocks, memorabilia, and coins that had been stolen.

So this had happened more than once. Wild. Was David Brown working at Leafbrook at the same time? I mean this could be a case of revenge, right? Instead of murder? Someone wanting to get their stuff back and killed him?

I was about to close the article when a name jumped out at me. One of the victims listed was Charity Valentine.

I knew her. Charity Valentine was a past client of mine.

There was a tap on my window. I jumped and stifled a scream. Some man was standing there.

"Hey you coming or going?"

I glanced to see his car pulled behind me, waiting to park.

"I'm just leaving," I said, biting off the "I'm sorry." I was really working on needlessly apologizing.

"Sure, no problem. I was just checking." He waved and returned to his car. I backed out , thinking about Charity. I knew where I needed to go next, and it wasn't to pull covers over my head.

7

Charity Valentine was a former client—my first client, actually—who I'd once clashed with and who had eventually become a friend. In her eighties, she was under five feet tall and just as cute as could be.

Her sister, Gladys, was warming up to me as well, although I'll admit, that was slower going.

I had a good idea of where to find Charity right now. She volunteered at the town's nursing home, and even when she wasn't running a game or a group, she was there visiting with her boyfriend. I hoped she'd have some answers about what happened with her safety deposit box.

I knew it would be okay to show up unexpectedly. Charity was always begging me to stop by and meet Henry, her boyfriend. In fact, I'd been delaying it. Been too busy with life... my leg.

I made a face, knowing I was hiding behind excuses. No, I needed to be honest, especially with myself. The real reason I hadn't visited was because nursing homes make me feel... strange. Intimidated, if I was being truthful. There was a part of me that was afraid that I'm going to come across a situation I wouldn't know how to handle.

I pulled into the Evergreen nursing home and parked. My hands instantly felt clammy as I stared up at the building. Feeling slightly ashamed of my reaction, I climbed out of the car and slammed the door. My foot throbbed as I hobbled forward, maybe punishing me for my nervousness.

This is going to be good. It will be amazing to meet this guy she's talked non-stop about.

I hiked up to the front door where a sign warned sternly in capital letters, "Do not hold the door open for our guests."

I swallowed hard as fear threw one final punch to my stomach, and then I grabbed the door and walked inside.

Ventilated air filled with the scent of hospital cafeteria food filled my nostrils. I pressed forward. The first person my eyes clamped down on was a woman sitting in a wheelchair next to the foyer window. Her head was crowned with a short white puff, and she wore a hospital gown with a throw blanket across her knees.

She smiled when she saw that I'd noticed her, her pale

eyes eager. "Come here. Come here." She beckoned, waving a thin curled hand.

I glanced around to be sure she meant me. Of course it was me. There was no one else around. I walked over, hesitation building as I entered an unfamiliar situation.

"What's your name?" the woman warbled, reaching out.

Her voice was so soft I squatted down to be sure I heard her. I gave her my hand. "My name's Stella."

"Oh, Stella." She nodded and her face crinkled into a smile. The wrinkles echoed the smile three or four more times across her cheeks. The tiny woman's hand was soft and frail, and the entire thing fit into mine like a baby bird. Gently, I held her hand, first feeling the cool of her skin and then a smidge of warmth from her palm.

I suddenly felt very protective over her.

As I stared at it, I was struck by a profound revelation. This little hand that appeared so fragile right now, may have been used to raise children or paint houses, change tires, cut fabric for clothing, make a million meals, and who knows what else. I smiled with a new appreciation. Who was she really?

She gazed at me like I was her new best friend. My tongue felt stuck in my mouth. Every question I had suddenly seemed scary. What if I said something that triggered sadness? Did her family visit? Was she happy she was here? I wasn't even sure if asking about her hobbies was shaky ground.

Start with the basics. "What's your name?"

"Dolly." The word came out with a breath but her eyes lit up. "It actually is Delores, but my baby sister couldn't say it so I've always been Dolly."

I grinned. "I love that name. It's beautiful."

"Beauty is only good if it includes your murmurs and thoughts."

"That's true. Are you sitting here so you can see the garden outside? It's quite colorful."

Her eyes took on a perplexed expression as her nearly hairless eyebrows rose. She glanced out the window, and I did too. I was disappointed to discover the flower garden wasn't visible from here.

"Can you see it from your room?" I prompted.

"My room is down that way. By the cafeteria." Slowly her hand rose again, and her curved finger trembled in the direction. "I miss flowers. I used to garden, you know."

"You did?"

She smiled and touched her fingertips together to demonstrate. "Roses like dinner plates. And oxtails, hydrangeas and the most beautiful lilacs. Not like the ones you see today. Mine were deep purple. Like an eggplant!"

"Really?" I grinned at the delighted sparkle in her eyes. I wondered if I couldn't find a sprig to bring her. "And what was your secret?"

"Flowers were different back then. More pure." She nodded sagely.

"I see. Well, I'm new to the area. So far, I've only managed to grow dandelions."

She nodded. "Dandelions are good for you! Grow them! Eat the leaves. I used to make tea out of them. When I was young I made wine." She put a shaking finger to her lips and her eyes slanted impishly. "The best wine you ever heard tell. Could get you goofy in just two sips."

I laughed. "Wow. Have you always lived in Brookfield?"

She shook her head. "No. I'm from Gainesville, up yonder. My daughter lives here. That's why I've come. To be close to her." She plucked at the knitted afghan across her lap. "I know just about everyone in these parts though. Worked as a school bus driver."

"Wow! A bus driver! You must have some stories then. Tell me more," I said. It wasn't a ploy. I suddenly felt like I was sitting on the precipice of hearing more wealth of experience than I could imagine.

"Oh, for sure. For sure. Some stories people might not want me to share." Her eyebrows raised slyly.

"How long were you a bus driver?"

She coughed softly and waved me away with a liver-spotted hand when I asked if she'd like me to get her a drink. She blinked her watery eyes as she recovered.

"I drove for years. Long enough to take my bus kids' children when they became old enough," she finally said. "Miss Dolly, they called me. Everyone knew me."

"That's amazing," I said, feeling relieved to hear her continue. She'd scared me with her coughing fit.

"Those kids loved me. They brought me presents, apples, a flower or a drawing. I saw more than one of them fall in love right there on that bus. Although, it wasn't always peace and pickles. Some carried on with the feuds their uncles had with their uncles, and their fathers with their fathers."

"You knew everyone, huh?"

"Just about. Of course, when the new people would come, we'd get the scoop on them pretty quick. Us drivers knew as much as the teachers back then. We knew who was a ruffian. Who was quiet. Who came from a troubled home. I'm here to tell you, those kids were the ones that bothered me the most. I always tried to have an extra smile and compliment for those. Who knew what kind of home I dropped them off into. There was one little girl who came every day with her hair a mess. Her momma had died, you see, in a car accident. I kept a brush and ponytails there just for her, and every day, I'd braid her hair. Cutest thing." Her eyes softened as if the little girl's face was still fresh in her mind.

"I'm sure you made a difference in so many lives."

"Isn't that the aim of us all? To make a difference? Make our mark? Life slips by faster than a popsicle fallen on a July's sidewalk. Who we are, and what we love is the only thing that's going to last. Those kids remembered me even when they became grandparents themselves. Most of them grew up all right. Some twisted themselves like an ol' bean shoot around a piece of pokewood."

Her face lowered, matching her voice. This conversation was steering into a dark direction. I needed to figure out how to head it off.

I charged in a new direction. "I sell houses out here. In fact, I just got a new listing up on Reeter's Ridge. Have you heard of it?"

"Reeter's Ridge, yes I have," she continued. "I remember the family who built that house up there."

My spine stiffened.

She glanced out the window and her lip puckered. "Those people were a strange brew. The father worked at some chemical plant. Ran it I guess. Never saw the mother. Heard she divorced her old man and fled out of state. She was afraid of him, and maybe for good reason. I remember the little girl. Alice. She had the worst crush on this boy named Tommy Barker. He yanked on her hair something awful." Miss Dolly chuckled.

"Did you know there were two houses up on the ridge?"

"Yeah, I did. The Elder Mr. Brown had his sister living in the other one. Spinster, I guess. We saw her from time to time but she kept to herself as well. Last I heard, she died of a heart attack, left the house to Alice. Don't know what happened to Alice. The house got sold to someone, I suppose. And the boy, David, I heard he's gone too. Shot by some crazed hunter." She shook her head. "So many gone before their time."

"Did you ever meet the dad?"

She waved her fingers like she was trying to dislodge a piece of fuzz. "No, never did. Never cared to. He caused an uproar when he pulled his kids from school. Said he was going to teach them himself. Strange man. Too many secrets going on up there."

An orderly walked up to us. "How are you doing, Dolly?" she asked.

The woman next to me cringed.

"Miss Dolly," I corrected, patting the woman's hand before standing back up. My leg throbbed as the blood returned to it.

"Oh? Is that right? Do you want to be called Miss Dolly?" The orderly smiled.

It was a subtle movement, but I swear I saw a slight straightening to Miss Dolly's bowed back. She glanced at me with a smile and then looked at the orderly. "That would be lovely, Dana. And how was your day so far?"

"My day is wonderful! Are you ready for dinner?"

"Have a good night, Miss Dolly." I waved.

She vaguely waved as the orderly unlocked the brake and pushed the wheelchair away.

"Stella O'Neil! What are you doing here?" A high pitched giggle came from the opposite end of the hallway. I turned to see Charity Valentine tottering toward me.

The short woman wore a pink dress, with her gray hair bobbing in fat sausage curls that she'd worn ever since I'd met her. She carried a pile of folders.

"Hi, Charity! I'm here to see you!"

"Me? Well, how wonderful!" she gushed, grabbing my arm with her spare hand. "You're just in time to meet my beau, Henry! I just have to drop these off at the front desk. Come along!"

I followed her to the reception area where Charity passed the folders over to the gal sitting behind the desk, then the little woman dragged me down a hallway that smelled like a cross between a minty cleaner and chicken soup.

"You will just love him," she insisted from somewhere near my elbow. Her feet, decked out in a pair of Mary Janes, pattered next to me. "He's the bomb!" Her eyes opened wide as she dropped what I could tell she felt was a fancy word marking his worth.

I grinned. "I can't wait. Hey, I had a question for you. I'm working with a client who was embroiled in the nasty affair up at a bank. While I was doing some research, your name came up as one of the people affected by the safety deposit boxes. Do you have time to talk about that?"

"Oh, that horrible swindling snafu? You'll have to ask Gladys about it. She knows everything. Now, here we are!" Like an overgrown Tinkerbell, she dragged me into the cafeteria.

Mr. "The Bomb" himself was seated at a table with two

other older gentlemen. The table's laminate surface was covered in cards.

"Ah, my love," he said, reaching a liver-spotted hand out to Charity. She released me and sprang over to smother his cheek with kisses. He endured the affection in the same way as one receives kisses from a puppy.

Finally, she finished. "Come, pull up a chair and sit," he said, gesturing to an empty chair next to him.

"I can't right now. I'm right in the middle of organizing tonight's Bingo, Henry. I just wanted to introduce my friend, Stella."

His eyes locked on to mine, and I instantly felt I was being weighed. Then he smiled and tipped his head. "Did you meet a resident named Dolly?"

"I did," I said, a little unsure.

"Dolly was just here to get her dinner, chattering a mile a minute about the most wonderful talk she'd had with a Stella. I assume that was you?"

Blushing, I nodded.

"I like your friend," he said simply to Charity, who beamed with pride. He patted the chair meant originally for Charity, and I sat down. Slowly, he dealt me thirteen cards which was how I learned I'd be playing the next hand.

We played Hearts for another twenty minutes—and I lost horribly—while around us conversation ebbed and flowed like ocean waves. It was relaxing. I liked it.

Finally, it was time for me to go. I headed out after saying goodbye to my new friends.

It was interesting how the day turned out. Back in my car, I ruminated over the conversation I'd had with Miss Dolly. I'd enjoyed talking with her and slowly pulling parts of her story out.

I realized that, as I'd listened to her share her life and how she'd helped so many people, something inside of me had been given a dissatisfied shove. It made me realize I desired a bigger story for myself, with loftier goals and more adventure.

And my heart yearned for someone to share it with.

8

The next morning I woke up with two messages. One from my dad saying he loved me and hoped all was well.

The other was from a realtor saying she was unable to open the Brown house for a showing because the box was jammed. So, right out of the gate, I had a chore to do to go bring up a new box.

I made a cup of coffee and grabbed my laptop. I wanted to learn a little bit more about the Brown family before I headed out there. For instance, what had happened to Alice, Mr. Brown's sister?

As my screen glimmered on, a red email notification reminded me of the scheduled visit to the Ashmount penitentiary tomorrow.

Mom.

I rubbed my neck as a kaleidoscope of emotions swept through me. I'd had so much going on lately, I'd put all my mom thoughts in a box to deal with later.

Dad was coming to the prison with me this time. This was a big deal since he hadn't visited her in all of these years. He'd tried one time, but then had chickened out, half due to a panic attack he'd never admit to having, and the other half due to a mixture of guilt and fear. I was hoping with fingers and toes crossed that he'd be successful this time. I think he needed the visit more than she did.

I sipped my coffee and then typed in, RandCo builds houses on Reeter's Ridge.

The search led me to an old Gainesville newspaper where I found an article entitled, "Architectural Delight or Eyesore?"

The article outlined how the Browns had built the houses back in the fifties. There'd been a small protest that they'd be destroying the view with two houses at the mountain top. A protest that seemed to have died down pretty quickly with the start of the Vietnam War. As I continued to search it seemed that the elder Mr. Brown had died and the house ownership moved on to Alice and David.

Neither of the Brown children had married. I wondered how the house was eventually sold to Charlotte Taylor.

Remembering that Charlotte had said she'd only lived there a few years, I searched for the MLS listing.

What I learned chilled me to the bone. Just like Mr.

Brown, that house had been sold by the same trustee, Mr. Coleman.

That meant Alice Brown had died as well.

Interesting. I shut the lap top and finished getting ready. My first stop was at the realty office for some open house flyers, and then I drove up to the Brown house. The new lock box rattled in the seat next to me.

There was a paper stapled to one of the mailboxes—Charlotte had posted a lost cat sign. Maybe she was hoping the realtors could keep an eye out. I made a mental note to check around as I turned into the driveway.

After I parked, I stared up at the porch roof, wondering where the birds were. The feathered rock fiends were no where in sight. Still, I hurried up the stairs where I fiddled with the lock with my key card. Like the realtor said, it wasn't working. My leg ached, and I finally gave up and sat on the stoop.

"What's the problem?" I pushed the box forward and examined the back.

Scrape marks marred the card reader. There was no doubt that someone had sabotaged it.

There was a key hole at the bottom, placed there for just this reason. The only key that worked was the broker's. I jimmied it in and got the box opened to rescue the house key. After replacing the lock box with a new one, I carried the open house flyers into the house for a look around.

That weird scent grabbed me by my nose again. What was it? Musty... like an old garage.

My gaze landed on the counter where there were several realtor cards scattered on the surface. So the lock had worked for a while before someone busted it.

Who would have done that? And why?

A rattle at the sliding glass door made me whirl around. My boot cracked against the counter with a loud bang, and I grabbed the corner to keep from falling. I tensed, preparing to do a clumpy sprint for my life when I saw that it was a broken branch scratching against the glass as the wind blew.

I set the broken lock box on the counter and rubbed my neck, feeling my blood thrum through my veins. How does this stuff happen to me? I couldn't wait until this place had sold. It might take weeks, months even as the market slowed down because of the approaching winter. Was I going to be able to handle this for months?

Okay, I needed to get a grip, and get it now. The sun shone through the windows and should have made the room light up. Instead it highlighted all the foot traffic in the carpet and a few smears on the sliding glass door. And what was that? Someone had let their kids eat gummy candy in here, and there was a wrapper and a few stray gummies frolicking on the carpet.

I briefly wondered if I should get the cleaning company out here again. Instead, I opened the cupboards in search for cleaning supplies. Finding window cleaner and a rag, I tackled the smears. After that, I scooped up the garbage. It reminded me of the soda can I'd found outside, that I'd thrown during the attack of the killer birds. I probably needed to track that can down again.

The trustee told me there was a vacuum in the closet, which I located and hauled out. I did a few light sweeps across the carpet to try and blend in the footprints. Then, armed with the cleaner, I headed downstairs for a quick check.

I didn't know what I would do if I found the carpet a mess downstairs. There's no way I was carrying the vacuum down, not with my leg nearly healed.

Luckily the carpet was neat from footprints. I spied a little vacuum plugged in the corner by the desk. Weird, I hadn't noticed it before but it was a smart thing.

I pulled the curtains back in the family room's window and admired the outside. From down here there still was a gorgeous view of the valley. I leaned against the sill and looked out.

I squinted suddenly. At the top of that tree down there, was that one of the crows?

Please no, please no. I was so hoping they'd gone home, disappeared, migrated, or did whatever it was that crows did for the winter.

Behind me came a thump. My blood instantly felt like firecrackers were going off in it. At the same time, my muscles froze. That was no branch. I couldn't look behind me.

What was that noise? Was someone here?

It's probably nothing. I had to be imagining it. Being alone in this house was doing things to me.

Bump, bump.

My pulsed drummed in my ears. Nope! It was real! I heard it that time, I knew it! Slowly I turned, armed only with a stupid bottle of window cleaner.

Nothing was there. Nothing behind me. Was something sneaking down the stairs?

Another thump, heavy and solid. Coming from the bonus room.

I searched around for another weapon, and finally snatched a stapler from the desk. These were the lamest weapons in the world, but you better believe I'd bean the stapler off of someone's head and squirt them in the eyes if they came at me.

The sound of soft footsteps could be heard from behind the closed door. My heart galloped in my chest. I had to move. Get past the door and get upstairs. Now. Don't look. Just get out of here.

Slowly, I edged toward the stairs. All I could picture was the door swinging open and some person coming out. Trapping me. I could barely breathe, I was so scared.

Please be brave. Move, Stella, move!

My leg felt like it weighed a thousand pounds in the boot.

The stupid heel squeaked. Surely he heard it. He was going to come out. I knew he was. He's going to open the door and catch me standing here with the stapler.

Just then, the door knob jiggled.

Truthfully, I nearly passed out from fear. My arm jerked back, ready to let the stapler fly.

The door knob stopped. *Don't freeze now, Stella. Baby steps. Keep moving. If that door opens, run as fast as you can.*

I continued to edge along the carpet. Almost past the door. Almost there.

But why did the door knob stop moving? Did they know I was out here?

I wasn't going to wait to find out. I grabbed the top railing of the stairs and took them two at a time, boot and all. The skin on the back of my neck crawled. I could just imagine the door swinging open and someone with a gun bursting out.

I was half way up the staircase when I heard something else.

Something definitely not human.

9

I reached the landing and waited, panting.

There it was again. A cat meowing.

What in the world? Was it really a cat? How could it have gotten inside?

Slowly the situation hit me and I started to calm down. Seriously? I was this freaked out over a cat in the house?

The flyer for the missing cat floated through my mind. I covered my face and groaned. I was an idiot. Panicked myself yet again by assuming the worst.

Still, I was nervous to go back down the stairs alone. But who to call? Who wouldn't laugh at me?

I bit my lip for a moment and then dialed.

"Hello?" Georgie answered.

"I need you to be my wingman," I said.

"What's going on?"

"Do you have a minute to keep me company while I go check out a weird noise in the house?"

"Of course! You need me to come over?"

"I'm not at home. Actually, I'm at the Brown house up on Reeter's Ridge. I heard a weird noise in one of the rooms, and freaked myself out until I heard it meow."

"Meow?"

"Yeah. I think it's the neighbor's cat. But, just in case it's not, I want company."

"Okay, you got it. Go check."

I glanced at my weapons and decided, of the two, the stapler was the better choice. Cautiously, I crept back down the stairs, arm cocked to staple a forehead if need-be.

"You okay?" she asked in a tight voice. I got it. I felt the same way.

"Yeah," I whispered. I'd reached the door by now. My hands trembled. Just got to gear myself to do it. Do it now. I reached for the doorknob and stopped, chickening out again.

"You sure?"

"Yeah," I said, and threw the door open.

A gray tabby sat just inside the room. Relief flooded through me, making my legs more wobbly than any shot of alcohol had ever affected me.

"Hello," I said. I may have been hanging on to the door frame, trying to recover.

The cat blinked golden eyes and stood up, floofing out its rather magnificent tail. He was sauntering past me when I finally jerked into action and scooped him up. There was a feverish moment of juggling, but I soon had the stapler returned to the desk, the phone pinned against my shoulder, and the cat firmly cradled in my arms. He seemed happy to be out of the room and relaxed like a heavy beanbag.

"Hello?" Georgie asked, her voice raising. "What's going on?"

"I've got the cat." I was still a little breathless. "I'm going to bring him back home now. I know where he goes."

"Good grief, never a dull moment in your life."

"Yeah. Maybe I should take Saturday off to relax," I hinted.

"Nice try."

"I owe you one." I laughed.

"Any time. I'm a good trouble wingman," she said, and we hung up.

I shuffled down the porch steps with a nervous look up at the gutter. Still no birds. Maybe I'd seen something else down in the trees. The cat was as motionless as a stuffed animal in my arms, aside from his paw with its little toe beans pressing against my shirt.

"Your mama is going to be happy to see you," I said, kissing his head. I walked past the mailbox and grabbed the poster. "Look. It's your picture! You're famous, buddy."

The cat sniffed the paper and looked away, seemingly unimpressed at his likeness. Maybe he was camera shy.

I headed down Charlotte's driveway, getting my first

glimpse of the front of her house. It was startling to see how much alike Mr. Brown's house it was. I don't know why it surprised me. After all, they were made by the same builder so that only made sense.

Like the Brown house, this one also only had a few deep-set windows on the front of it. It had the same long concrete porch with wrought iron railing. I hobbled up the steps, the cat purring in my arms at recognition of his home. I rang the doorbell.

There was no answer. I waited a minute, wondering what I was going to do now, should she not be home. Should I take the cat back with me?

Just then the door opened. Charlotte limped out, hair in a towel and a bathrobe on.

"Oh! Gus!" she yelled, scooping him from my arms. And then to me, "Where on earth did you find him?"

"Believe it or not, he was in Mr. Brown's house."

"Gus! You naughty boy! Whatever were you doing over there?"

"Maybe he snuck in during one of the house showings."

"I'm not sure. He's an indoor kitty. He never goes outside, Do you, boy? You had me so worried. I didn't even know he was missing until last night. I've been beside myself. You don't know how to live outside, do you Gussy?" She glanced at me. "I honestly thought a cat burglar had taken him away."

I pressed my lips together just in time to stop the smile. She didn't realize what a cat burglar was. At the same time, her statement struck me as curious. "What made you worry about that? Have you seen someone in the neighborhood?"

"Oh, tons of people."

I figured she was referring to the realtors. "I mean, besides house hunters."

"Sure. There's been a sneaking cat burglar here many times in the last year. I've called the police a million times but no one ever does anything about it."

Whoa. "Have either of the houses been broken into? Who have you called?"

"Mine's been okay. Every time, they send out a police officer, the same young kid. He's never found anyone around when I call. Of course, he takes so long to get here. The last time I called they said I needed to up my own home security."

"Did you ever do that? Put up your home security?" I couldn't help but wonder if this prowler was the one that shot Mr. Brown. Did she have her neighbor's death on tape?

"Yes, I did. I had to. And I've been watching the tapes all day to see who took my baby." She smothered kisses on the cat's head. Gus laid back his ears. His twitching tail showed he wasn't happy.

"And did you see anyone?" I prodded.

She shook her head. "Not unless you count the ghost."

"Ghost? What ghost?" I gripped the handrail, not at all sure of what I was getting myself into. Charlotte, sweet Charlotte, was suddenly coming off a little delusional. She even said that the police had quit taking her seriously, and that was saying something.

She brushed her hair off her forehead in a very casual way. "Rebecca. She comes around at night sometimes. Moves things in the house. I've even seen her down the embankment by the white pipes."

"You've actually seen her, then. Have you ever tried to talk to her?"

"Oh no. You're not supposed to contact spirits. Besides, she doesn't cause too much trouble."

"Wow. Okay. Did you ever ask Mr. Brown if he saw her?"

"Don't you remember? I never met my neighbor in my life."

That's right. She had said something like that.

She continued, "By the time I moved here, he was already a recluse. Like I said, I just saw deliveries being made and such. I didn't want to bother him."

"Just you and the ghost..."

"Exactly. Until the other person started snooping around."

"Did he disappear like the ghost, too?" I asked.

She looked at me like I had just grown a pair of antlers. "Don't be absurd. People don't disappear."

"Well, I mean, you said the cop never saw him so..."

"By the time the cops got here the person had already driven away."

I rubbed my head, trying to track this conversation. "So you called the police on the man snooping. Not on Rebecca."

She smiled then. "When I hear you say it, it all does sound kind of crazy. And here I am in my bathrobe. But yes. That's right."

I was relieved she had some self-awareness of how it sounded. It gave me more faith in her story. "So, what kind of car was he in?"

"Well, I never saw the car." She pointed down the road, with Gus looking interestedly. "I assumed that he parked down there."

"Would he come to your property?"

"No, mostly he'd poke around Mr. Brown's. I was worried he might steal my cat though. Huh, Gus?"

"Is it possible that your security camera caught him? Or, as horrible as this sounds, maybe Mr. Brown's death? Maybe we could prove it was a hunter?" Or someone else.

"No, it never did catch him. And then he stopped coming around. Which is good for me! And good for Gus too, huh, baby?" She kissed the cat again, ignoring his flattened ears.

"Is it possible to show me what you recorded on the camera?" Then, realizing she had obviously just stepped out of the shower. "I mean, if you have time. I'm kind of interrupting you right now."

She laughed and her eyes lit up. "I know. You caught me being a lazy pants. I'm a night owl now so I shower later than I should. But come in! I can't believe I've let you stand out here all this time."

She walked away, leaving the door open and me with no choice but to follow. I walked in and immediately gasped.

Her home was much cozier than Mr. Brown's, and a sweet smell of vanilla seemed to underscore it. But the view! The view was just as breath-taking, maybe even better.

"I made some banana bread. Would you like a slice?" She already held the knife over the loaf and was cutting.

"Sure." I grinned.

She slid it on a plate and then licked a crumb from her thumb. "Try it," she said. "I'll just go run and get dressed and get the video."

I carried the plate to the picture windows. The view immediately dragged another "Wow," out of me. I shook my head, impressed, and took a bite of the moist bread. Warm, sweet, and a touch of cinnamon. I practically whimpered.

Now what had she said about pipes being down there? I squinted but couldn't see anything from this height.

Movement behind me made me turn, and I saw Gus staring at me. He half-closed his eyes in a cat smile, before strutting over.

"How did you get over in the Brown house?" I asked, holding out a crumb.

He gave it a disinterested sniff.

"Try it. It's good!" I coaxed, thinking, "If you were a dog, you would have taken off my finger by now."

The cat allowed me to convince him and he sniffed it again, this time taking the crumb in a delicate bite. He licked his lips which seemed to prompt him into giving himself a complete face wash. I scratched his ear.

"Isn't he adorable," Charlotte said, entering the room. Her wet hair was slicked back into a ponytail and she had dressed.

I straightened up, noting a pang in my back. Was that little bit of house cleaning that strenuous on me? This foot issue had completely knocked my exercise regime out the window, and I'd seemed to replace it with one too many pints of ice cream.

And bacon burgers, I remembered guiltily. Regardless, it

was unfair how quickly I could get out of shape. I needed to get back on track.

"He totally is. And this is delicious." I crammed in the last bite. I'd get back on track tomorrow. Maybe.

She carried a laptop over to the counter and then helped herself to a piece of bread. "Would you like something to drink?"

I shook my head. "No. I'm fine."

Taking a big bite, she booted up the footage. "This is actually all I have. Tell me what you think." The screen was grainy, with layers of gray and black that I was used to seeing in night surveillance footage.

Then a figure moved across the scene. I leaned forward, senses prickling. There was definitely someone walking around.

Despite the pixelated image, you could see it was a woman. She wore a white dress and appeared glowing in the moonlight. She moved in an ethereal way, almost as if she were floating. I rubbed at the goosebumps that had risen on my arm.

"Meet Rebecca." Charlotte dropped the words so frankly that I found myself nodding my head. But could it be really? A ghost?

"You call her Rebecca. How do you know that's who it is?"

"Oh, I don't. But if we have to share this space together, she had to have a name. I couldn't just say, 'Yoohooo! Please leave my toilet paper alone! And turn off the lights when you leave the room!' She needed a proper name so I call her Rebecca because she reminds me so much of a character in my favorite book. Her presence is felt everywhere."

"She does those things? With the toilet paper and lights?"

Charlotte nodded, popping the last bite of bread into her mouth. She nodded toward the screen. "Watch. This is when she leaves."

I turned back to the video. The woman seemed to float down the property.

And then she disappeared.

I gasped and grabbed the corner of the screen. The clock at the bottom continued to tick but the woman never reappeared.

My jaw dropped open as I lifted my head. "How often does she come by?"

"Oh, once a week or so. Sometimes several times a week. She's due for another visit soon."

Gus meowed at Charlotte's feet, and she lifted him up.

"Do you think you can call me when you see her again?"

"I'd really like that. I've been sitting on this alone for so long, it would be nice to have another set of eyes as a witness," she said, letting the length of the cat's tail run through her fingers.

"Good. And call me if you see anyone else messing with Mr. Brown's house. We'll figure this out."

I gave her my number. Her fingers flew across the keyboard and my own phone vibrated.

She'd texted,—**It's me** with a smiley face.

I grinned, partly wondering what I'd gotten myself into.

"Thank you for sharing that. And the bread. I need to head back and lock up the house."

"You text me if you need anything." She shut the laptop.

"I will. And I look forward to your call about Rebecca. Take care now," I said as I walked to the door.

The last thing I saw was her holding the cat's paw and making him wave goodbye as I closed the front door.

She was a nice lady. As far as that video went, that was the weirdest thing I'd ever seen. What could it have been? Someone pranking her? But the figure disappeared.

I'd never believed in ghosts, but I knew a lot of people did. Maybe there was something to this.

I shook my head as I entered Mr. Brown's place to make sure everything was secure. It was spooky after the video. "Rebecca, don't be gracing me with any visits," I said out loud. That declaration didn't make me feel better. I hurriedly put the cleaning supplies and vacuum away.

Just before I left, I stood in front of the sliding door. I could just see a hint of Charlotte's garden from here, along with most of the huge rhododendron bush still festooned with a few unseasonal red bell-shaped flowers.

What was going on over there? I thought about Alice, and how the house had been sold to Charlotte through a trustee. I mean... could the ghost be Alice? A draft tickled my neck.

I turned to check the front door and was surprised to see

it shut. All the rest of the houses' doors were shut, and the windows were locked. I knew because I checked every single one of them.

There it was again. An icy tickle wafting through the air. I licked my bottom lip and glanced one more time at the neighbor's garden. The shrub's leaves shivered as if feeling the same draft.

I needed to leave right now. Silly or not, I couldn't handle being here anymore.

But when I got home, I'd search to see if any weird crime had taken place at Charlotte's.

Specifically to a woman.

11

I left the Brown house intending to go straight home, but instead decided to make a detour to my favorite place to brainstorm.

My grandfather's house.

But first I needed to stop at the bakery for a bribe.

Oscar was grumpy, and gruff, and could be unpredictable. He was also wonderful.

Thirty minutes later found me thus sugar armed, standing on his front porch with my hand raised to knock. It was not necessary. Through the dirty paned glass I could see Peanut, my grandfather's Pomeranian, tearing around the corner in response to the sound of my footfalls up the steps.

She barked like her life depended on it and jumped to see me out the side window. Unfortunately, it was almost too high off the ground for her, so she was only able to make a quick peek every four or five jumps or so.

"Hi Peanut!" I waggled my fingers at her, which elicited an extra piercing yip.

A moment later, Oscar appeared around the corner. He wore his usual uniform of red flannel slippers, baggy jeans, and a button-down shirt that had seen better days.

"Bear!" He yelled. He insisted on calling the pup Bear, spurning the name his late wife had given the animal as 'too sissified.' "Be quiet, you little orange corn nut! What am I going to do with you?"

He scowled as he stared through the window, his eyes big behind his thick glasses and his hair two gray tufts of tumbleweed sprouting over each ear. "Stella?" he asked.

"Yes! It's me. Open the door."

"Confounded dog, you nearly tripped me and made me land on my flamboozle! And then where would you be? Who'd give you treats, then?"

There was a metallic fumbling at the frame and then the whole door shuddered and finally it was open.

"Stella!" Oscar grinned. He rubbed his whiskery cheeks before holding out his arms. "Where have you been, girl?"

He welcomed me in with a warm hug and quickly whisked the cookie box from my hands and was heading with it into the kitchen before I had time to shut the front door.

"So what's new in the fishbowl?" he asked, automatically getting out a mug and going over to his ancient carafe.

"It's been weird, Oscar. Very weird. And I'm heading up to see Mom tomorrow. I still haven't touched base with Dad to see if he's coming. I'm kind of scared to talk to him in case he uses that as an excuse to back out."

"Mmm," Oscar said, his bushy eyebrows lowering. He set the mug in front of me and I took off the cardboard lid to the cookies. He filled his own mug and brought it back. Just before he sat, he tipped his head like he'd heard a little voice whispering and then shuffled over to the far corner of the counter. There, hidden in the shadows, he retrieved a powdered creamer container. He brought both it and the spoon to the table before landing down in the chair with a huff. Peanut promptly hopped up into his lap.

"Creamer, huh?" I noted. I'd never been offered anything but black coffee from the time I'd met him.

"Cecelia," he sniffed. Cecelia was the lady next door who ran a bed-and-breakfast and just happened to be Georgie's boss. She also seemed to be running in cahoots with Oscar, even going so far as to be referred to as "buttercup."

I ignored the creamer, not liking the way it made my tongue feel coated.

"So you're here for a talking moment," he said, using his quaint phrase he pulled out to mean a deep conversation.

"Yeah, I guess I am." I helped myself to a macadamia nut

cookie. Oscar watched with one eyebrow arched and then did the same.

"So this house I'm representing has been nothing but weirdness. Today alone the neighbor's cat was locked in a room downstairs and the lock box damaged. Yesterday I got yelled at by a waitress for not knowing the history of the house. I dug into it a little bit and I can't find anything super unusual."

"What did you find out?"

"I know that a developer from out of state was called to build both it and the house next door, presumably because the homes are on the cliff. Both houses have stayed in the family until recently. The mom moved to Florida, the aunt died of a heart attack. Both houses were sold to the original owner's children, Alice and David Brown." I paused for a second for emphasis. "And both of them are dead."

"Both!" Oscar jerked slightly. Peanut lifted her head, fluffy ears as pointed as they could be with interest at the cookies. Oscar absentmindedly smoothed them back, and she relaxed to return to sleep.

"Yes. Now David had to have some enemies. He was the inventory guy for a bunch of safety deposit boxes whose items went missing. He was investigated but there was no evidence for probable cause. Soon after that, he quit his job and became a hermit in the house. This very house I'm trying to sell." I chewed the inside of my cheek, before coming right out and saying what I really thought. "I don't think he was killed by some random hunter. I'm pretty sure it was by someone trying to get their stuff back. But I can't prove it. And I'm afraid if I don't figure it out, it will be a secret that he takes to the grave. There's no one left who cares."

"Well this is starting to sound like a maze of mirrors. Where's the house again?"

"In Gainesville. Up on Reeter's Ridge." I hesitated. Should I tell him about the video Charlotte had me watch? The one with the ghost? I decided not to. He didn't ascribe to spooky supernatural things. He was a fact man, being an ex-FBI agent, and it would probably derail this entire conversation and his train of thought.

"You know what, I'm curious now. And I want to have an answer should Tamra come at me like that again. I'm calling the builder." I grabbed my phone and did a quick search.

"Are you now?" He nodded sagely with a cookie in his hand.

"Yeah. I'm not sure what's going on, but my antennas are telling me something's off." I found the name, RandCo, and quickly dialed it.

"Your antennas," Oscar scoffed.

I waved him off and glanced at my watch. It wasn't closing time yet. Hopefully someone there would answer.

Nerves clenched my stomach as I listened to the phone ring. What would I do if they didn't answer? What would I do if they did?

"Hello. RandCo Construction. How can I help you?" a pleasant woman's voice answered.

"Hi, there." My mind went blank. Oscar stared at me like I was his favorite sit-com, and happily crunched on his cookie. What do I want to ask? Stall! "I—uh—I have a question about a couple houses you built."

"Okay, sure. Where are the houses located?"

"In Gainesville. There are two next to each other."

There was a long pause. "We don't build in that area. Are you sure it was us?"

"It was in the fifties."

"Oh! Well, in that case, I can't help you. This company has changed hands multiple times."

I groaned. "Okay. Thanks anyway."

"Well, I might have something helpful for you. One of our general contractors retired quite a few years back, but he worked at this business since the beginning. Maybe he can help. He's actually from that neck of the woods."

Hope flooded through me. "Terrific! What's his name?"

"Clive Farmer. I hope that helps."

I noticed she didn't offer a number, and I was a little nervous to ask. I mean, I was really poking my nose in here. Still, I swallowed my nerves and tried my best. "If it's not a privacy issue, I'd love to talk with him. Do you have a way to reach him?"

She paused for a moment and my hope raced again. But, in the end, it was what I expected. "No, I'm sorry. I can't do that. Check the white pages. You might find him there."

With that we hung up.

"Well?" asked Oscar. Peanut rested her chin on the table to watch me, blinking sleepy eyes. Her eyes sharpened as she caught the scent of the cookies.

"I have a name, no number. She did say he was from this area so I'm going to check."

It was so long ago, I had no idea if the man was still alive. I hit the white pages with the name. Moments later several entries rolled up.

My mouth dropped. I never expected to see the name that I did.

12

"What's going on? What's the matter?" Oscar picked up my shock right away.

"It's the list of names!" I understood now what the problem was earlier. I couldn't believe it hadn't occurred to me then.

"What is it?" Oscar asked again.

"There is a Clive Farmer listed. And underneath it, it says one possible relative is Tamra Farmer." I looked up. "I bet that's Tamra from the restaurant! Clive must be her dad!"

"How old is she?" Oscar asked.

I wrinkled my nose, trying to think about that. "Thirties maybe?"

"More like Grandpa," Oscar answered. "Didn't this take place in the fifties?"

"Yeah. You're probably right. Her Grandpa then. She

must be close to him." Heat rose in my cheeks and I shot Oscar a guilty look. We'd only met recently. I'd grown up not even knowing he was alive, thanks to my father's estrangement.

That was in the past. And Oscar seemed to think the same thing. "We've got lots of time to create bonds. You keep bringing the cookies and it'll go quicker."

I snorted and went ahead and dialed Clive's number. I was coming off a high of discovery and with that came courage to ask strangers weird questions. What did I have to lose?

"Clive Farmer speaking," was the way he answered. No hi, no hello, no gentle breaking it in. His voice was gruff like he chewed framing nails and spit them in the wood.

It seemed obvious he was related to Tamra.

"Hi, this is Stella O'Neil," I answered back. Wow. I sounded twelve. Buck up, girl! "I just got off the phone with Randco with a few questions about a house built back in the fifties. Actually two houses, up on Reeter's Ridge? They gave me your name and thought you might know the answers. I looked you up in the phone book. I'm sorry to bother you, but I was wondering if you had any time for a couple of quick questions?"

I heard him exhale. Not once, or twice, but like there was a bull about to charge on the other end. Then, silence. I stared at the screen to make sure we were still connected.

"What sort of questions?" he finally asked in the same gravelly tone.

"Well one thing I was curious about was I heard there were pipes at the bottom of the property. White ones, I think?"

"I know we put in a drainage and vent system that comes out at the bottom of the hill. Always drips water."

"So you remember it then. Terrific. It's for drainage?"

"Yeah. sure. A place like that needs special shafts for water and air, among other things. Common with a steep grade like that. Keeps the ground from eroding in the rain. Without them probably the whole house would come down after a few years."

His words underlined my entire questioning of why someone would want to live like that. "You think the house could come down? No. Don't answer that." I immediately regretted the question and hoped desperately he wasn't about to tell me something I'd be forced to reveal to a buyer.

"Nah. We put in a ton of stabilizers. Honestly, everything was normal except for the foundation. Weirdest substructure I ever saw."

"Weird how?" I hated that word being used as a descriptor over a house I was selling.

"Weird like it didn't seem to fit the house. But people want what they want. And the Brown family wanted those houses."

"Can you describe in what way it didn't fit?"

"In a way that gave us trouble getting permits. I'll tell you right now, the town wasn't too happy about the houses being built. But I'm darn proud of them. Eventually someone greased enough palms, I guess, and we got the permits we needed, and had those trees down and the forms for the foundations up before a fortnight was over."

"Very nice," I said. "Did you go on to build elsewhere in the town?"

"We built everywhere." I heard the sound of a lighter and then a deep breath. "We done here?"

"Yeah. Thank you very much."

I didn't have all the words out of my mouth before he had hung up.

"Well?" asked Oscar.

I twirled the phone on the table. "I guess my questions were answered. I mainly wanted to know about the pipes. They're normal, part of the drainage system."

"Why are you frowning then? Sounds like you got what you needed."

"The guy said something odd about how the foundation didn't match the house being built."

Oscar took a swig of coffee and hummed. "Stella, the guy is the same age as me. Maybe older. At my age, you just don't remember stuff like you used to. Maybe it was one of the first houses he built that was on a cliff. Maybe it needed more support than he realized."

I nodded. "Could be true. At least I know the pipes are

okay and not something I have to reveal as a structural issue."

"This world has a lot of questions, a lot of drama, and a lot of controversy just waiting to tear you down. Everything wants to rip you out of your happy place. You got to fight to stay there and not let anything distract you."

"What are you saying?" I asked, confused.

"I'm saying that mind of yours is always working overtime and you need to give it a break. Sell the house. Live your life. Be happy. Quit all the poking around and giving needless worries any headspace. It's like gambling against the house in Vegas. Trust me, it doesn't pay out well."

I studied him and realized he was giving good advice.

After all, he would know.

13

I didn't stay much longer at Oscar's after that. I needed to get home and get some rest. After all, I had a big day to prepare for.

And part of that was sending Dad a message that I would be picking him up at six the next morning. It had taken me a minute to know how to word it, but I decided no questions, just a straight forward expectation. I figured I wouldn't give him any way to wiggle out of it, especially through a text message. He sent me back as a string of emojis. I studied them for a minute, trying to figure out what they meant. Finally, I decided he figured he'd try them all, assuming at least one of them would be right.

The next morning, he was ready when I arrived outside his hotel. He'd flown in from Seattle especially for this moment, and I was proud of him. He stood under the hotel awning, his skin the same shade of gray as the early morning light.

I had a cup of coffee for him, and I handed it over after he climbed in.

"Thanks," he said, with a weak grin and buckled up.

The nutty coffee scent filled the car as I started out for the prison. It was over an hour away and the drive was silent and surreal as we headed in the direction of the rising sun. The rays slipped over the horizon with long pink fingers, only to be hidden again as we drove up the mountain pass.

We were about half way up when I first noticed it; a tremor in my hands that seemed rooted straight in my chest. At the next bend, my heart leapt into my throat. My lungs locked tight like I'd just run a marathon, and I realized I'd been holding my breath. I started to pant, and the breaths came faster... faster. The sensation was so unexpected I nearly threw up.

Dad's gaze flicked over to me. He didn't say anything. I think he was trying to figure out how to ask what was going on.

"I—have to pull over," I gasped.

"You okay, Stella?"

I shook my head, my vision abruptly becoming blurry with tears. Luckily, I found a spot where the shoulder widened, and I quickly pulled in. I switched off the car and dropped my face into my hands. Sobs tore out of me, unexpected, yet so expected.

"Aw, sweetie. I promise I won't back out of the visit this time. I swear it." Dad's hand patted my shoulder awkwardly. Despite his own freak-out the last time we were here, he wasn't used to huge emotional displays. Everything that had happened recently had knocked both of our stable worlds for a loop.

But he was wrong, that wasn't the problem. I tried to get the words out, yet, suddenly, I was too tired. I reached for the steering wheel and squeezed, overwhelmed with lost words. How could I explain that I didn't know this car? That this was just a rental I had to use until my insurance doled out the money for a new one? This car wasn't my baby. This one was a stranger.

My baby was the car that had saved me.

"What is it?" he asked gently. "What's the matter?"

His tone was the same as the time he'd comforted me as a child after a horrible nightmare, and years of trust that Daddy would beat back the monsters freed my words.

"Th—this is it, Dad. This is the road where my car crashed."

Dad cringed. "Sweetie, I'm so sorry. I've been so wrapped up in my own drama I totally forgot. Here, you get out, and I'll drive."

I shook my head. "No, I'll do it. I just wasn't expecting to react like this." That was an understatement. I knew it would be hard, but I was completely caught off guard at the visceral response my body had to the memory of the trauma. It was almost as if it were acting as a separate entity from the rationalizing of my brain.

You can't hide from trauma, you can't fool your body that it's over and it didn't happen. You can't talk yourself out of it. I was starting to wonder if the only way to heal was to march right through it and realize you were worth the journey.

"You sure you don't want me to drive?"

I wondered if he might be worried about his own safety. "I'll be okay. I want to do it. I want to face this."

"Okay. Take your time. You're in charge of how this goes."

I loved my dad so much. I smiled at him and took a few more breaths. Yeah, something horrible happened to me here. But I survived it. And I was going back to face it on my own terms.

I flipped on the signal and, after making sure no cars were coming, I pulled back onto the road. The next few turns weren't easy. I can't say I didn't cry, I did.

Dad just whispered, "You're incredible" and patted my hand.

I tried my best to control my breathing. In through the mouth, hold it for the count of six, ease it out the nose for the slow count of seven. I did it over and over as images of trees flipping, flashing red-and-blue lights and the screech of metal railing splitting replayed in my head.

I made it. God got me through. I'm here now. I repeated it with every exhale.

We came around the last corner and I knew exactly

where I was. Here. It was here. I slowed down to see it, the place where I almost died. The place where I'd come to terms I would die. Where regrets flashed through my mind and promises were made that I would live my life differently if I survived.

You couldn't even tell an accident had happened. There was a new guard rail and new painted lines. Everything looked pristine.

Except for the tree. A monstrous behemoth, it had held my car from tumbling the rest of the way down the mountain face until the firemen had arrived. The tree stood proudly, appearing just as strong, and at first glance, you might have thought it was just the same as well.

I slowed even more and stared at the beautiful tree. Down the bark was a long scar, hardened yellow now from dried sap. A wound it had healed from, but the healing had left its mark as well.

Tears welled in my eyes again. Grateful tears.

I might have scars as well. Scars that one day would remind me that I was strong, that I had healed.

"You okay, sweetie?"

"That's where it happened."

Dad turned and looked. "What did you see then?"

"I saw pain and fear."

"What do you see now?"

"I see beauty for ashes. Answered prayers."

Dad swallowed hard and his Adam's apple jumped

several times. I could see he was having a hard time keeping it together. I thought for a moment to tell him that I was okay and not to worry. Then I realized he might have to face his own pain and fear too. And he might need my support to march through it himself.

I patted his hand this time. "I love you."

He looked at me and his eyes were wet. "I love you, too." Then he turned to stare out the window where the sunrise finally conquered the top of the mountain to shine a soft lemon light onto the guardrail. It flashed next to the car as I continued to drive.

We were almost there. The both of us.

14

I showed my credentials at the prison gate and bit my thumb nail. Everything in me hoped this would be the last time I needed to do this. The guard stared at it for a long time, and for a moment, I worried that he wasn't going to let me in. Irrational, I know. But, I always feared that when I came here.

Once again, I was anxious for nothing. He handed my license back with a nod. "Have a good visit," he said, lifting his hand to the other guard to raise the gate.

It rose and we drove through, my car jogging over the speed bump.

"Well, this is it," Dad said, staring at the building. His eyes were so wide I could see the whites around them.

That is, they should have been white. Right now his eyes were bloodshot from the earlier emotions leaking out.

He must have suspected the same. "You have any eye drops? I bet mine are so red, they could call a bull in."

"I'm sorry, I don't. But you look okay." So, I lied. I knew he was already frazzled.

"You're fibbing, I can tell. You looked away," Dad said glumly.

I smiled, my lips feeling as stiff as cardboard, and we got out of the car. The morning air greeted us, crisp with the rising dew. Chirping overhead dragged my gaze upward to where a bird had landed on the light pole. With jerky motions, it looked this way and that before stretching its wing and lifting up. The little wings flapped again and again as it rose higher and higher, up over the prison, over the trees. Until it was a black dot. Until it was out of sight.

How many prisoners watched the same sight and longed to be just as free?

I grabbed Dad's hand, and we walked up to the main gate. "It's going to be okay," I whispered.

He didn't respond, instead moved stiffly like a wooden soldier. I worried about him.

He exhaled deeply when we were buzzed in. Slowly, we made our way through all the check points. Dad's eyes bobbed around as he took in the other people standing in line with us. He swallowed hard, his lips pressed tightly together. Finally, we were permitted to wait in the final area.

This was it. The next stop was Mom.

I sat in one of the chairs. Dad joined me, uncomfortably

perched on the edge of the plastic seat as if it were a cactus. His hands squeezed together until the knuckles turned white under the skin, and then relaxed. His thoughts were probably tumbling around a million miles an hour.

I'd been there myself.

I also knew there was nothing I could say that would make this better. He had to sort through it himself.

I rubbed his arm to remind him that he wasn't alone and then pulled out my phone. To distract myself, I scanned to the MLS and saw the open house banner was scheduled to show up tomorrow on the listing. Good.

When I glanced back at Dad, I noticed he wasn't as jittery. Instead, he stared intently at a young mom with a baby.

He noticed me watching and turned to whisper, "Who watches the kids?"

"I'm not sure. I guess they go back, too," I whispered back.

The baby started crying, and the mother shushed it with a sing-song. Baby was bounced up as the mom moved rhythmically; pat, pat, pat, shush, shush, shush. Finally, the baby calmed and leaned against the mom's shoulder, his fat little cheek squishing to the side. His eyes, like twin olives, stared into mine.

Pat, pat, pat.

Shh, shh, shh.

Slowly the baby's eyes closed. They flicked open to half moons and then closed again, his body relaxing. It was fascinating to see the smooth operation of the mom who hadn't looked up from her phone the entire time.

Do all mothers rock like that? Gently back and forth, like it was second nature? I was tempted to try it, just to see how it felt.

"Stella O'Neil, Steve O' Neil," a loud voice called.

Dad jumped next to me like he'd been hit by a live wire.

"It's okay, Dad," I whispered.

We got up and walked through the green metal door where we were immediately enrobed in stale air. The last buzzer sounded, and we entered the remaining room, the one with the plexiglass with the flowered holes drilled through so we could talk to the person on the other side.

I sat down and pulled Dad into the chair next to me.

"Where is she?" he asked, his hand gripping the counter before us.

"They're bringing her right in." I reached for his shoulder and started patting.

After a second, I smiled.

Pat, pat, pat.

Shh, shh, shh.

Maybe it would come naturally to me after all.

The door slid open with a gritty metallic sound like sand was caught in the hinges. In came the guard, ushering in Mom.

Mom. My heart lit up.

It was different than the last time I'd seen her, when

she'd skulked in like a kicked dog with her head hanging. This time, her head was up, her hair was back, and— my eyebrows shot up in surprise—was she wearing makeup? But how? I knew they didn't allow it in there after putting money on the books for her commissary.

Her eyes locked onto Dad's and then I really wondered about the makeup. Dad made a guttural sound somewhere in between a groan and a yawn. His mouth hung open, he could have been doing either one. His eyes stretched as if seeing color for the first time.

I wondered how she appeared to him, now twenty years past. And how did he look to her?

Her eyes were calm, drinking him in. Inquisitive.

"Vani, you look amazing," Dad finally breathed.

"Steve, you look nice yourself." She sat down. "Sorry, I'd shake but...." Here she lifted her hands to show the handcuffs.

Dad grimaced. "You'll be out soon, I hear."

"They've sped up the parole hearing. It should be next week. I'm glad."

It was incredibly unfair that she had to go to the hearing, but between the choice of a new trial or parole, this was faster. She would get a new trial soon, but the first goal was to get her out.

"Stella, I'm so glad to see you." Mom nodded to me.

"Me, too, Mom." I smiled.

The anticipated awkward silence descended between us. I bit my lip, wondering if I should break it.

"I got your letter. Thank you," Mom said to Dad, her gaze watching him intently.

He blushed red and shifted uneasily in the chair, making the bolted legs squeak. "There aren't enough words."

"I understand. We'll talk more when I get out, but for now you need to know that I've moved on with my life as well. And I don't hold any grudges. Life is a crazy mixed bag and we either make the best of it, or we let it grind us down to a nub."

Dad's eyes softened. He sighed. "I did my best with our girl."

"Hey!" I said. "I'm right here." Maybe I shouldn't be? Their eyes were locked in a pretty intense way.

Mom smiled at me. "Of course you are, my little angel."

This was weird. Bizarre. They were both treating me like I was a little girl. Almost as if they had been transported to some mutual memory they shared together before any of this happened.

I didn't protest any more. This healing had a life of its own. Maybe they had to start in their past to be able to move forward together to the present day.

I would have even given them some time alone. But, there was nothing I could do until the guard came. I couldn't even scoot the chair away since it was bolted to the floor. So we'd deal with it.

As I dragged my attention from my inner thoughts, I could see maybe they already had. They had moved into another conversation without me about some memory from the past. Mom was smiling. So was Dad. Everyone had relaxed.

"How is Oscar?" Mom asked.

"Oh, he's as grouchy as if he had toast crumbs in his drawers," Dad said. His eyes crinkled at the side.

Mom laughed, looking ten years younger. "You remembered!"

"I'll never forget when you said that. It was after you first met him and—"

"And his chair fell back, pulled over from that heavy leather coat!"

My gaze danced between the two of them. Okay, this was weird. Ten minutes together, and they were finishing each other's sentences. What was going on?

They talked for every bit of the forty-five minutes allotted to our visit. I mostly listened. I learned more about how life was in that time when I was a baby, than I ever had in all the years in between. Stupid things—it seemed they were purposely keeping the conversation light—like where their first apartment was, and how they'd lost the keys to the hotel on their honeymoon night. I saw real reluctance in both of their eyes when the guard returned for Mom. She told me she loved me and held her hand against the glass, our ritual for goodbyes.

And then she held her hand out for Dad.

He matched it with his. "We have more to talk about. Real stuff. I appreciate you letting me back in to talk with you at all."

"We'll get to it, Steve. Being in here has really taught me to take things one day at a time."

"See you, soon, Vani."

She was escorted through the door. When it clanged I saw Dad jerk, almost as if he'd been woken from a dream.

"You ready?" I asked.

He nodded, and we headed back through the cold cement maze to the sunshine waiting for us outside.

"Can I do this?" he murmured, almost to himself, after we'd climbed into the car.

"Do what?" I asked, while digging around for the seat belt.

"Make amends? Isn't it all too big?"

"You're doing it, Dad. You're facing the mistakes and owning them. I'm proud of you."

He leaned back against the seat. I noticed him glance at his ring finger and rub his thumb against it thoughtfully.

A strange thought occurred to me. "Dad, when did you two get a divorce?"

He didn't answer, instead gave a goofy grin.

"Dad?" I asked again. The pause was getting ridiculous at this point.

"We never did. We're still married."

My jaw dropped open. "What?"

"I ran, Stella. I ran and never looked back, convinced she'd cheated on me. I couldn't deal with the betrayal and locked it away."

"How could you lock it away for so long?" I asked.

"I don't know. I didn't mean to. Life happened, and I kept busy and by the time I thought I was ready to deal with it, life had grown stable enough that I didn't want to wreck it by bringing up all that pain again. It was a horrible decision. I'm sorry. It turns out, you really can't run from your problems. They have a way of finding you no matter how far you run."

My mouth opened and shut more times than a fish out of water. I didn't know what to do with this news. I'd have to unpack it later. I shifted the car into gear, and we drove home, our silent drive loud with internal thoughts once again.

15

Mom and Dad were still married. *Dude.* I was about as prepared for that little nugget of news as Chicago was ready for a volcanic eruption. I didn't even know where to go from here.

It bothered me all night. I tossed and turned, first it was too hot, and then too cold, and then I had to pee. I finally gave up around six and headed downstairs for an extra strong cup of coffee.

Mug in hand, I settled down at the table to scan the internet. Georgie had texted me, just a sweet reminder about the shindig later that day. I wrote her back that I was kind of in a weird mood.

I was surprised when she answered, she must be up early too. Her text made me smile.—**Weird means you're my people! Let's just have fun and forget about everything.**

Maybe it could be fun.

I watched the birds at the feeder and drained the coffee from the mug, not even feeling a bit of enthusiasm to go host the open house on Reeter's Ridge. Time was ticking away so I dragged myself to the shower. In there, I remembered that I'd be seeing Richie and his date, so I spent a longer than usual amount of time shaving, plucking eyebrows, and applying makeup.

I checked myself in the mirror, actually feeling pretty cute. Then I hobbled out to the car for a planned stop at the bakery. After grabbing some goodies, I drove to the realty office for their huge coffee carafe and then made my way to the Brown house.

I stopped at the fork in the road and placed my little A-shaped Open House sign. The light was weird, with the sun shining in that thin way again, making the shadows appear paler than usual. Was it because we were so high up?

I pulled into the driveway, and sat for a moment, staring at the house as the engine ticked softly. The thought of the ghostly lady in the video made my skin crawl. I remembered the closed door from a few days ago, and every bit of me screamed not to go in there.

I reached into the bakery box for a frosted cookie and took a bite, chewing fast. Sugar always was a good battle weapon against fear.

Let's get it done. I shoved the rest of the cookie in my mouth, got out, and popped the trunk. With the most unladylike grunt, I hauled out the second Open House sign and propped it at the end of the driveway. I grabbed the cookies and beverage basket. It was a juggle to get everything up the porch, and I was sweating like a hog by the time I ran my card under the key pad. I unlocked the door, half afraid of what I'd find inside this time.

Dim, cave-like light welcomed me. And that funny smell, too. Why were the blinds shut again? I needed to leave a note to remind the realtors to leave the blinds open and the doors shut. Somehow they were getting things mixed up.

I hoped it was them.

I hauled the food and beverages to the counter and started the coffee machine. I hadn't brought flowers, knowing the fake ones were here, but I did have cute napkins and a candy bowl. When everything was in place, I set out a notebook with a pen, hoping to get all the guests' names as they came through.

Stepping back, I surveyed my work. It looked as well as it could be. I glanced at my watch and saw there was still time left. I needed a quick tour through the house to check on the bathrooms (you never knew when a client forgot to flush) and open all the blinds.

I checked the first room and scooped up a paper coffee cup someone had left in the sill. I hated when people left garbage behind. I hurried into the master bedroom and stopped.

A thin wailing sound came from the living room.

What. Was. That? I peeked around the corner.

There it was again! I held my breath to listen. Was it coming from the front door? Outside? I'd heard that before, but where? Had it been in the video Charlotte showed me?

No that wasn't it. Some horror flick? I never watched them—too scary. In fact the commercials made me cover my eyes. That had to be it.

The thin wail started up again. No. That wasn't it! My heart hammered in my chest. Then the windows shuddered from a blast of wind, and the roof creaked.

It's the wind! The memory of wind blowing down the gutter came to mind. I was freaking out about wind gusts.

I sunk to a crouch and held my forehead. I was a hot mess. I didn't even want to confess to myself the thought that flashed through my mind was that it was David, looking for justice.

Ever since I'd stepped foot at this place, before even, when those darn crows were pelting me, this place had me rattled. I needed to get a grip and get it fast.

Feeling like my heart had slowed from a gallop to a slow trot, I stood up, brushed my hands off and fixed my hair, and then headed downstairs.

I was happy to see the doors were shut and the window blinds left open down here. I had to admit, despite my conviction to keep my imagination chained to the curb, I eyed the bonus room with a little shiver.

Peeking inside, I was relieved to see it was empty.

Everything is normal, save the wind and a coffee cup, you big goof. Satisfied, I was about to head upstairs when my gaze landed on the huge desk.

That's right. I hadn't had time to finish exploring it. For instance, what was that key for that I'd found? I checked my watch and pulled out the drawer.

"Hello!" a man called.

My heart sank that someone was already here for the open house. I shoved the drawer back and managed to croak out, "Welcome!"

I'd be back to deal with this later.

Soon the house was overrun with potential buyers to the point that I couldn't keep an eye on everyone.

I remembered Kari telling me that at every open house there were looky-loos who were just curious. Some people even made a date of visiting open houses and dreaming. Like that couple over there. Holding hands and pointing out fixtures and treatments like they were trying to impress me they were truly interested.

I smiled.

But what about that couple over there? The man's red hair tufted from his scalp like a bed of sea grass. They didn't look happy at all. She was dressed to the nines, and he looked like it had been an effort just to roll out of bed. The woman had a grip on the man's arm and was whispering furiously at him, while his gaze bobbed around in a weird way.

As I watched, the couple disappeared into the other room.

Call it a hunch, but they were up to something. I could tell. I followed after them only to be stopped by another person. "I've heard about this place," he said with a wink.

"Oh?" Why was he winking? "What have you heard?"

"I mean, Mr. Brown owned it and we know all about him. Have you found any treasure?"

"Treasure? There's no treasure."

He was dragged away by his wife before I could question him further.

I rubbed my neck. These were the people Mr. Coleman, the trustee, had warned me about. I managed to escape the group of most of the onlookers, only to pass someone in the bathroom who was saying, "What do you think? Should we open all the drawers?"

This was rapidly getting out of hand. I searched in the last room for the original couple. Where had they gone off to?

They had to be in the basement.

I snuck down the stairs and was about half way down, when I heard whispering. I froze, clinging to the handrail, afraid to take another step in case a creaking tread would give me away. My hands were sweaty, and I could only imagine how this would look if they appeared around the corner. I'd look ridiculous, that's what.

"It's got to be around here somewhere. There were sixty of them, and they're all gone."

"You think he sold them?" the woman asked.

"Sold them? I would have heard about that. They're not something that can disappear that easily."

"Well, apparently they can," she hissed back.

"This house is weird enough, he could have hidden them everywhere. Check behind the picture frames."

"What about the bricks in the fireplace? Should I try to pry any out?"

Okay, that was my clue to move if there ever was one. I continued down the stairs, making sure I pounded my feet. When I rounded the corner, the two of them smiled at me, just as innocent as could be.

"How are things down here?" I asked.

"Oh, good. Lovely home," said the woman. The man raked his hand through his hair, making it stand up even more if that were possible.

They faced their backs to me to examine the view out the window and slowly moved away. They couldn't be more obvious about wanting me to leave them alone if they had a sky writer.

That wasn't going to happen. "So, have you two been looking for a home for long?"

The woman turned back, surprised. "I suppose. We're new to the area."

"If you'll excuse us," said the man, with a firm, fake smile.

"And what were your names?" I asked, completely acting like I hadn't heard him.

They glanced at each other, and the man answered for the both of them. "Sam Smith. Mr. and Mrs. Smith."

"Interesting! Let me guess, do you know Will and Jada?" My inner voice snorted. Would they get the joke?

They stared at me blankly and if anything the corners of the woman's mouth turned down even more.

"I'm kidding." I said.

"Mm," the man hummed and turned away again.

This was as awkward as chaperoning two teenagers on a date.

They walked down to the windowless bonus room. Like a blood hound, I stayed on their trail.

"So, this isn't a bedroom since there is no window. Housing regulations say every bedroom needs an escape if there is a fire. Technically, this is a storage room, but it could make a nice office or studio. Do either of you record or paint?" At this point I was babbling.

The man stared at me blankly but there was nothing I could do. I wasn't about to let them alone to tear apart the place.

"If we could just have a minute," he asked again.

"Of course, but it will have to happen upstairs. The open house is about to close soon and... "

"Close?"

"Yes, unfortunately I have to be somewhere else and have to close this early." I was grasping for straws at this point, reaching for any excuse. What if there were other people thinking about prying bricks? This was too big of an affair for me alone to watch over.

They made eye contact again and didn't appear pleased. Fortunately, they headed back upstairs. I trailed after them trying to mask the huge sigh of relief with a cough.

More people were here. As I walked through the kitchen, I noticed several cupboard doors open and a drawer left ajar.

"Everyone! At this time the open house is closed. Please sign the notebook with your contact information," I said, gesturing to the paper on the table.

Now where did the Smiths go?

I hobbled to the front window where I saw them speed walking down the driveway. Several other people followed. Carrying the notebook, I corralled the rest and shooed them out by asking for their information. If there was one thing people did not like to do, it was to give someone access to pester them.

Soon, I had the house empty. I limped to the end of the driveway and removed the open house sign.

Okay. New marketing strategy. I couldn't take a risk of that happening again.

After cleaning the upstairs, I headed back down for another sweep. The house didn't feel spooky now, just annoying that it wasn't selling. What were the Smiths doing down here, anyway?

My gaze fell on the huge desk. I hurried over and glanced through the items on top, but I couldn't tell if anything was missing. I pulled out the drawer.

The same pen rolled along the bottom. Brushing it aside, I pushed on the false bottom. It opened with a satisfying pop. I pulled it away and peered inside.

It was empty. The key was gone.

16

My mouth dropped. This wasn't just a case of an over-active imagination about a cat getting in, or drafts shutting doors. That couple actually had rifled through this house and stolen the key.

But why? There was nothing around here with a keyhole. I looked around some more but didn't see anything else obvious that was out of place. What were they doing?

I mean, it was plain to see they thought there was something stashed here that had been stolen from the safety deposit boxes. But why focus in the basement? The only thing down here was this desk and a folding chair in the bonus room.

A deep pain throbbed in my head. Great, a headache was coming on, and I only had a short time to get back home, clean up, and head back out for the dance. I briefly thought about canceling, but I couldn't bring myself to do it to Georgie at such a late notice. Besides, one thing I knew about me, as much as I hated the idea of going someplace, I usually enjoyed my time once I arrived.

Georgie must have picked up my vibe through osmosis or something, because my phone rang before I was even back in town. I answered it, remembering how much she hated to text.

"You still coming?" Her voice rippled with suspicion.

"Yeah. I just need to go home and get a pain pill for my headache. Then I'll be on my way."

"Aw, rough day?"

"I had an open house."

"Oh geez. Lots of people show up?"

"For a while there it was pretty crazy. But really it was one specific thing that happened that made it so bizarre."

"What was that?"

"This couple I caught snooping around. They were so suspicious." I snorted. "They even gave me a fake name."

"Oh I have to hear it. What was it?"

"It's so stupidly obvious. A Mr. Sam Smith."

"Sam Smith? Does he have red hair?"

What? So that was a real name? And here I'd thought they'd given me fake ones. "He did have red hair. Oh, my, gosh! That really was his wife?"

"No, he's not married. At least not that I know of. He did, however, used to work at Century Bank. He used to hit on me when I first moved here. His pick-up lines were the worst. A few months ago he gave me all the details of his recent Lasik procedure. 'Eyes like an eagle,' he said. 'Can spot a perfect ten like you a mile away.' And then he winked at me." She made a gagging noise.

"What a freaking small world." He worked at a bank? I had to look this up. "Listen, I'm almost home. You need me to bring anything tonight? I mean besides my sweet ax skills."

She laughed and said no, and we hung up. I raced inside as fast as my booted foot would let me and yanked out my laptop. My fingers flew across the keyboard like the keys were too hot to touch.

First, I typed on social media to see if I could find him. I gave up a half second later. Apparently, there were like thirty thousand Sam Smiths.

Next, I typed in Sam Smith and Century Bank, hoping some employee page would pop up.

That was a big fat zero.

What did come up was a banner ad for Century that said, "Proven over one hundred years." With a smiling face. I gasped.

That smiling face was the Mrs. Smith. His fake wife.

So she worked there or at the very least was an actress that had been hired to appear in the ad. One way or another, she knew Sam Smith and the bank.

The infamous bank, I reworded. I glanced at the time and

groaned. I was running late. And I really wanted to look cute tonight in case I ran into Richie.

I stared at my boot ruefully. It is what it is. I limped upstairs, did the armpit sniff test of my shirt, changed it, put on a spritz of my favorite perfume, hit my hair with some dry shampoo and was on my way.

The barn hop was pretty easy to find. There were tents and a giant air man and a field filled with cars. I parked the car and climbed out.

The crowd was huge, and I hesitated about jumping in there. How was I ever going to find Georgie? Filled with dread, I texted her that I was here.

She called back immediately. "Come to the red tent. Do you see it?"

I did see it and hobbled in that direction.

"Stella!" a man called. Richie approached me with a very cute, very petite, and very blonde woman on his arm.

Terrific.

I felt like a hulking monster with my huge boot. And, despite my shirt change, I still felt sweaty. Not to mention I had forgotten to double check in the car that my makeup hadn't smeared. Probably had raccoon eyes at the moment.

I smiled and double blinked. "Hello!"

"I can't believe you made it! You said you couldn't dance so I figured you'd probably not show up. Maggie, this is Stella, Stella, Maggie."

The woman did a spritely one-two step. "I love dancing."

My smile felt like it was made of plaster and was undergoing an earthquake. I fought to keep it from disintegrating. "Well, normally, I can dance. Now, however," I gestured to the boot.

"Oh, what happened?" the woman asked. "That looks horrible and clumsy."

My gaze flicked from her back to Richie. "Well, it was nice seeing you."

"You here all by yourself? Why don't you hang out with us?" He turned to the woman. "She's new here and doesn't know very many people."

"Aww," the woman sighed, with a decidedly pitying expression.

"I'm meeting friends," I said with a determined nod. "You two have fun."

"All right. If you're sure. We'd love to have you." Richie grinned.

The woman's eyes slanted, letting me know that was not a mutual feeling. "You be careful now. Don't get hurt again."

"Run along," I said, making a shooing motion. I walked away from them with my head held as high as I could, considering the darn limp made me feel like a wayward camel.

Red tent, red tent. Just get me over there.

I saw Georgie before she saw me. When she spotted me, she smiled like I was a celebrity and waved her arm in welcome. I can't tell you how good that felt.

"Hey, lady," she said when we finally closed the gap. "Glad to see you. This place was boring! Want a cherry?" She held out a bag of cherries.

"Boring, huh? I could use a little boring," I said, taking a couple.

She shook her head. "No, you need a burger and a beer. Come on, let's go."

The area around the tents was packed with people. There was a large empty space to the right of us with hay bales set up. At the end was a covered stage with a band playing some smooth honky-tonk music. The singer was talented with a skilled bass accompanying him. I took in the scents of barbecue and the smiling faces—some a little redder than others after a long visit to the beer garden—and started to relax. Georgie was right. This was good for my soul. I popped a cherry into my mouth and peeled out the seed, then launched it into the grass.

Then I spotted him.

"Oh my gosh! It's him!" I said, grabbing Georgie's arm. My blood felt like an ice floe in my veins.

"Who?" Georgie asked, her eyebrows raising and the freckles on her nose bunching as she squinted.

"That guy over there. His name is Gary Studebaker. He's the first person I showed the house to." He wore the same dirty t-shirt or one very similar, and his greasy hair lay in the same comb-over. I had no idea why the sight of him caused this reaction, but my every nerve was creeped out.

The man walked over to the starting line and grabbed an ax from the wooden bucket. He took a sideways stance in front of the target and rolled his shoulders back. Then, with a stare down at the bullseye ring on the hay bale, he cocked his arm back and flung the ax.

It sailed over the bales with a chorus of whistles and laughter from the surrounding audience.

"I think the goal is to hit the target, Gary!" one of the men yelled. Gary gave the man a dirty look before grabbing another ax. This time he did a few practice moves. One. Two. Three. On three, he let it launch.

The ax hit the center of the target with a thud that made everyone cheer. I shuddered.

"He is pretty creepy, isn't he?" Georgie noted. "And you were alone with him?"

"Uh huh," I nodded.

Another guy walked up, tall and very broad shouldered. He grabbed an ax, making his back muscles flex under his tight shirt. I instantly straightened and made a casual fluff of my hair. Now there's someone I could get to know.

"Who is he?" I asked Georgie. "He's cute."

"Who, him? That's my boyfriend, Frank."

Where are sinkholes when you need them? I blushed and stammered out an apology which she quickly brushed off.

"How would you know? I've never introduced you. What a turd, he didn't let me know he was here already." She checked her phone to be sure. "He's not good at that stuff. By the way, he's friends with Carlson. He actually used to work with him, but now Frank transferred to state patrol."

"I should have known. He has matching grouchy eyebrows just like Carlson."

She snorted. "Yeah, he kind of does."

We watched as Frank tried to hit the target and winced when it bounced off. With a shrug, he turned away.

"Frank! Over here!" Georgie called, waving again.

His hand shaded his eyes as he searched in our direction. Spotting us, he headed over.

"Georgie," he said, pulling her in for a hug, his hand running down her back.

"Hey, I didn't know you were here," she said slightly accusingly.

"Sorry. I just dropped Grandma back at home and headed straight here. Then my phone died," he answered back. He pulled out his phone to prove that the battery was dead.

"I'm just kidding you. Anyway, this is my new friend, Stella. She's Oscar's granddaughter."

He squinted as he studied me. "You from Hollywood?"

I rolled my eyes. "Seattle. That sounds awful familiar, though. Did you hear that from Carlson?"

"Yeah." He stuck out a hand for me to shake it, which I did. "How do you like it so far?"

"Great!" I answered rather lamely. My mind was still

caught around the fact that Carlson had mentioned me to him. "How's Carlson's new girlfriend doing?"

"Girlfriend?" His eyebrows rose quizzically. "That boy hasn't had a girl since high school. Besides, the only girl I know he's interested in is—Ow!" He yelled, scowling at Georgie.

"Sorry, I lost my balance." She smiled back.

"Caught yourself with your elbow to my ribs, hmm?" he asked.

"Don't be dramatic. Anyway, Stella is watching that guy over there." She nodded in the direction of Gary. "He came to one of her house showings and started snooping all over."

"What guy?" He turned to look. "Oh, I know him. I know all about him."

17

B oth Georgie's and my gaze snapped toward Gary, who was lining up his ax for another throw.

"Really!" Georgie perked up as I leaned forward. Who was that mystery man?

"He's one of the managers at the Century Bank. He was there when all that controversy went down with the safety deposit boxes."

"Seriously?" I stared harder. What was going on?

"That's why my only lock box is in my house. Bolted to the floor. And even that's not fail-proof." He squinted at the man. "We put the group of them through the wringer, however, they all came up smelling roses. It's one of those mysteries." He glanced at Georgie. "You okay for me to leave?"

"Go on. Have fun," she waved.

"All right then, I have to go defend my title." He wandered back to the ax throwing competition.

I stared at Gary. "He's got to be guilty somehow. I felt it that day he came by."

Georgie followed my gaze. "Maybe. He's got those shifty eyes. Not to mention he looks like he brushes his hair with a pork chop."

I laughed, and she grinned too.

"Come on," she said, pulling on my arm. "I'm starving. Let's go get something to eat."

We headed down the food row and considered our options. Pulled pork sandwiches, barbecue chicken, elephant ears, roasted corn on a stick, and Philly cheesesteaks. That sandwich was calling my name, and I was in line faster than a dog after a bone.

Georgie went for a blooming onion. I paid for my sandwich—mouthwatering with its fried onions and meat, oozing cheese— and met her at one of the picnic tables.

"So how did you and Frank meet?" I asked, before taking a big bite. Holy cow, this sandwich was good. I felt like I was on the second rung to heaven.

"I grew up around here. I was the bratty girl who hung out with the gang of boys on bikes and was better than all of them at kickball." She dipped an onion petal in sauce and chewed. Her eyes rolled. Apparently the onion was in a close contest with this sandwich.

"Stella O'Neil, fancy seeing you here!"

I spun toward the high-pitched welcome. It was Jan, the local postmaster at the Brookfield Post Office. Surprise fluttered through me to see her in normal clothing and not the blue vest with the golden eagle pin I was so used to seeing her wear.

"Hi, Jan! How are you?"

"I'm doing middling," she said and sat down with a heavy sigh. She turned to me with serious eyes. "More importantly, how are *you* doing?"

"I'm fine, almost out of this thing." I waved to the boot.

"Yeah? How's that Brown place going?"

I started and then grinned. I shouldn't be surprised. Jan knew everything about everyone. "It's kind of an interesting place, that's for sure."

She shot Georgie a smirk. "Interesting ain't half of it. The Browns were before my time, but I remember my Grandpa always used to say Gerald Brown was a Nazi war criminal."

My mouth opened so wide a swarm of bats would have been at home, while Georgie choked on her onion petal.

"You okay?" Jan asked.

Georgie took a sip of her soda and nodded.

Jan watched her, a bit suspiciously if you asked me, before continuing. "Anyway, that place was fated for bad things. It's no wonder David Brown was killed there."

"An accident," I managed to squeak out.

She smirked again. "Accident my foot. Someone was trying to get their goodies back. And maybe they did." She stood up abruptly, her short page cut wobbling. "Well, with that I need to go. Skittles is waiting and tonight's our favorite show."

Skittles was her cat. I numbly nodded, and she trotted away. Before she got twenty feet away, she was stopped two more times by people greeting her.

"How did she know all of that?" Georgie asked.

I smacked my forehead. "I'm such an idiot. Why didn't I ask her?"

"It's not often the phrase Nazi war criminal gets brought up at a hoedown. I wouldn't have been more shocked if a parade of juggling hedgehogs came strutting out onto the dance floor."

I rubbed my forehead, feeling the headache returning. "I'll look into it. Trust me, I'll figure it out. There's got to be something out there."

"I don't think it's real. I mean how true could it be? I've lived here my whole life."

The security I heard in her words sent darts of jealousy through me. She'd experienced a stability of living where everyone knew everyone else, and she was part of that group. "You're lucky to be in the same place you grew up in. All that rich history, everyone knows you."

"Well, it's not always that great. Besides, I think you are so brave, coming all this way across the country on your own. What a cool adventure. And it paid off in a big way! I can't believe you were able to find your mom." Her voice was weird, tight and unnatural, and she finished the sentence with a sigh.

I glanced at her curiously. Why the sigh? "I didn't even know she was missing for a long time, so I don't know how amazing of an accomplishment it really is. I feel like an idiot for not looking sooner."

She shrugged. "I don't see how you could have known. Your whole family was in on keeping the secret. You moving out here, I think it was your subconscious trying to get answers."

I bit the sandwich, thinking she was right about that. I had moved back to get my family together and get answers. And I was extremely fortunate to get both. "What about you? For some crazy reason, I thought Oscar said you had recently moved here yourself."

Her lips tightened in a way that let me know I'd hit a sore subject. Oh, boy. What had I done? Quickly, I tried to fix it. "You don't have to tell me."

"No, it's okay." A smile flickered across her mouth, the kind that was meant to put me at ease and had nothing to do with how she was feeling. "I actually worked for attorneys who sold auctions in Pittsburgh."

I swallowed hard. The job she had now was about as big of a career change as a person could make. I knew that meant something had happened. And from the tightening around her eyes, it wasn't something good.

"That must have been interesting," I said casually. It was

a throw-away statement meant to grease the wheels toward a different direction if she wanted to take the way out.

"It was. I really loved it. Working with antiques and the excitement of an auction." She stared at her fingernails sadly. "I loved my life back then."

A chill wrapped itself around me at the expression of loss in her eyes. It actually scared me, dug at my own pain I carried. I wasn't sure if I wanted to hear more. But I wanted to be supportive.

What should I do, now? Ask more? Sound interested? Change the topic?

I was still trying to decide when she continued. The words were unemotional and dropped from her mouth like the rhythmic clicks of a tally counter, "I was engaged to this great guy named Derek Summers. We were on the top of the world." She chuckled humorlessly.

My heart jumped to my throat. I knew what she was going to say next.

Except I didn't. It was much worse than anything I expected.

"He committed suicide in front of me. Drove his car off a cliff while I was following him." Her eyes swam with tears. She wiped her tears impatiently.

Her words felt like a punch to the gut. I clapped my hands over my mouth in horror.

She rubbed around her ring finger. "The problem with that was that Derek was not in the least bit suicidal." Her gaze met mine and her eyes were hot. "And don't try and tell me they can hide it. I knew him, and he was happy."

"I believe you," I whispered, blinking hard at the stinging in my eyes. How was she so brave and strong?

"Sorry. It's just been the run-around every time I tried to get answers. But I did find out some stuff."

"Stuff like what?"

"Stuff like Derek wasn't who I thought he was. He'd been working for a shady company called Midnight Trucking. And then I found out that Oscar knows all about them."

"Wow! What did Oscar have to say?"

She sniffed and grabbed a napkin for her nose. "Getting information from Oscar is like running on a waxed floor. Nearly impossible, don't you think? He was worried what I would do with it, that I'd get myself into trouble."

"He won't tell you anything?"

"Nothing really. Just dropped that little tidbit, and that's it. I was trying to figure out the key to unlock what he knows, but it's sort of been derailed. He's had his mind on other things, and I haven't wanted to bother him."

Heat filled my face. She meant me and all of my drama. "Oh. I'm sorry."

"Oh, my gosh! No! Don't feel bad!" she quickly said. She grabbed onto my arm. "Your family needed to heal, find out how to forgive. That's important too. My mystery helps no one but my peace of mind. My Derek... he's gone."

I tried to swallow over the lump in my throat. I could see

it in her face, and I wondered why I never saw it before. A haunting.

I shook my head, again amazed at how strong she was. And I knew she had moved on. But if there were answers out there, well, she deserved them.

"Georgie, this is a lot, and I don't know how you've dealt with it all this time. You are amazing. I promise you, after my mom gets out, I will help you get your answers. I'll work on Oscar, ply him with all his favorite foods, do whatever it takes until I get him to talk. He might be stubborn, but I assure you he's met his match in me."

She laughed. "I have no doubt about that. Look at all you've accomplished already. I really appreciate that. And same with you, if you run into problems, consider me part of your crew."

"We're about to rule the world," I said.

"You better believe it, baby. I was meant to rule."

18

The rest of the night was a blast. After a visit to the beer garden, Georgie and I were both laughing. Georgie and Frank took a turn on the hay-strewn dance floor, and even I attempted a spin or two, hobbling along with a cute grinning guy in a cowboy hat. I even saw Richie, and it didn't sting. I raised my hand to say hi and felt good about moving on.

I was exhausted when I returned home and practically dropped straight into bed. I'd just turned out the light, punched the pillow a few times to make it have the right shape, and rolled to my side when the phone rang.

I listened to it ring and groaned, knowing that the effort of getting out of the warm bed and answering it was going to take away any possibility of sleep for a long time.

I heaved myself up, squeezing out a wheeze, and hobbled

over the cold floorboards, mentally berating myself for leaving the phone on the desk.

"Hello?" I answered, my voice husky.

A breathless voice answered back, the energy jerking me awake. "Stella! She's here! Rebecca's in the garden!"

"Who's here? Who is this?"

"It's Charlotte! Remember the mystery lady in white? She's here right now. You have to come over!"

"Uh, yeah! Okay. I'll be right there!" I hollered back, not considering the feasibility that the ghost would still be there when I arrived. I shimmied into a pair of dark sweats and a warm hoody. At the last minute, I grabbed from the bottom of my sock drawer my dad's ski mask that he insisted I take and my new mini pepper spray.

As I scooted to my car, I texted Georgie. Sure, she was probably asleep as well, but I thought it might be nice to have some back up.

She called me back rather than texting. "Are you serious? Ghost woman? I'm totally there. You want to pick me up, or have me meet you?"

"I can swing by and get you. I'm on my way now. Wear dark clothes."

"You got it." She paused. "It's too bad I can't get Frank's night vision."

"You think he'd loan it?" I asked.

"Oh, I'm sure he'd loan it, but then I'd have to tell him what I wanted to use it for. And there's no way I want to endure that lecture, especially at this time of night. He's extra grouchy when he doesn't get his beauty sleep."

I laughed. "We'll be fine. I don't expect we'll get any closer than Charlotte's top deck. I'll see you soon."

Twenty or so minutes later, I was driving past the brick apartment building that Georgie lived in. She was already downstairs, skulking by her gated entry way. By skulking, I mean she was dressed all in black, including a knitted beanie and dark gloves. I was surprised to see no one had called the cops on her.

She scooted into the car when I pulled up.

"Hi!" she said, as she buckled up. "You ready for this?"

"As ready as I'll ever be!"

Ten minutes later, I turned up the mountain drive and entered the black abyss. The moon was hidden by clouds and the car headlights cut weak stripes in their losing battle with the darkness. I hit the high beams and kept my eye out for leaping deer.

No deer, but a skyful of moths. I'd never seen anything like it. They fluttered in the twin swatches of light with silvery wings like a living snowfall. Unbelievably, they didn't hit the windshield, instead they swooped and dove in their own perfect storm.

And then, the next moment, we were through them and they completely disappeared.

I swallowed but didn't say anything. The car was filled

with that muted stillness that happened at night. Even the music playing from the radio couldn't battle it.

The higher we went, the mistier it got outside. I had to slow down even more to be sure I didn't miss my turn.

"Creepy out there," Georgie said, startling me.

I squeezed the steering wheel and nodded in agreement. A few minutes later, I slowly pulled over by the mailboxes, the gravel crackling under the tires. I couldn't see anything beyond them, visibility cut to fifteen feet by the thick fog.

Georgie glanced at me, her face an unnatural paleness from the lights on the dashboard. She didn't say anything, and to me, appeared like she regretted saying she'd come.

I called Charlotte. "We're here," I whispered.

"So is she," she whispered back. Her words made my skin crawl with goosebumps. "Where did you park?"

"I'm by the mailboxes. Where are you?"

"I'm heading down now. I didn't want to be standing outside by myself."

We hung up, and Georgie eased her door open, an action that was a thousand times braver than I felt. "Let's do this," she said.

"Ghost busters!" I hummed. She snorted, my brave friend returned, and I opened my door too. It was a moment of levity, but once outside in the swirling mist, my mouth dried to a crisp. Carefully, I leaned against the door to close it.

Just then, a pale figure drifted around the bushes. I

squeaked. It was meant to be a full out scream, but fear choked it back.

It was a good thing too, because as the figure came closer, a light flashed in my eyes.

It was Charlotte, appearing every bit as freaked out as I felt.

"She's still there!" she hissed. "Hurry."

"Do you think she saw your flashlight?"

"I didn't turn it on until I saw your car. I wanted to make sure you knew it was me and not some ghost."

Just then, Georgie rounded the corner, appearing rather spectral herself as the mist parted around her dark figure.

"Charlotte, this is Georgie. Georgie, Charlotte."

Awkward introduction at best, but we were on the hunt for a ghost so it was the best I could do on short notice.

"You ready?" Charlotte whispered.

The three of us scooted down and scurried forward, hugging the ground. I pulled my ski mask from my pocket and yanked it on. I relished the barrier from the cold air against my skin. It actually made me feel safer.

At the first hedge, we all paused. A branch cracked on the other side of the thick foliage. I froze, we all did, like ice sculptures at a wedding.

The sounds stopped.

Charlotte glanced back at me and squealed.

"What? What?" I yelled, swinging around to see behind me. Georgie did the same.

Charlotte staggered back, grabbing at her heart as she wheezed. "Your face...." she panted.

Oh, my gosh. I'd forgotten she hadn't seen me put on the mask. "I'm sorry," I whispered.

Georgie groaned. "That probably scared every living thing away from mice to the Sasquatch."

"We aren't looking for a living thing," I reminded her.

Silence descended between us. "Let's keep going," I said. Charlotte nodded, her eyes still wide with fright. We crept forward again.

There was nothing behind the bush. We followed Charlotte around the side of her house to the yard overlooking her garden.

"She was down there." She pointed.

It was hard to see anything with the fog. We stood there for a minute and all stared out to see any movement in the pea soup. The mask grew moist. Finally, I yanked it up so I could breathe.

"I don't see anything," Georgie said.

"Me, either," I agreed.

Charlotte's shoulders slumped. "She's gone."

Well, that was a bust. "Now what?" I whispered.

"I'm not sure." Poor Charlotte's mouth dipped, making her appear both disappointed and confused.

"Let's go back to your house and watch your camera."

She nodded. The three of us crept up to her front porch.

Charlotte didn't turn on the lights when we were inside. I

wasn't sure if that was comforting or not. She disappeared down the hall, her lame leg making a dragging sound. Georgie and I glanced at each other and she shrugged.

I walked over to the window to stare out. It was impossible to see anything beyond the deck. It truly looked like a black abyss.

But just because I couldn't see anything didn't mean there wasn't something staring back at me.

Then I saw it. The woman in white. She was floating a few feet away on the other side of the glass door, her face lit in a blueish glow. My ears buzzed as adrenaline shot through my veins.

"Look at this." Charlotte said unexpectedly at my shoulder.

I jumped so hard there was a moment there I may have appeared at heaven's pearly gates. In the next half-second I realized the apparition in the glass was Charlotte's reflection. She carried her laptop, and the screen glowed against her face.

"What is it?" Georgie asked.

Charlotte turned the screen so we could see it. In the camera footage there was nothing but blackness.

I rubbed my neck, still recovering from being scared half-way to Sunday. "What does that mean?"

Charlotte pressed her lips together. "It means someone knocked down the camera. Watch."

She hit rewind and the screen jagged with static. Then

she pressed play again, and we saw movement. It looked like tree branches moving in the wind. There was a shot of the moon and then something white, like a glimpse of an arm. Then the screen went blank.

"Someone knocked down the camera right then," she said glumly. "Someone who knew I was watching."

19

As a group, we decided not to call the police. Charlotte had already been warned previously they wouldn't come up without direct proof, and we all decided that it was possible a branch falling in the wind was responsible for knocking down the camera. In fact, after staring at the screen for a while, Charlotte was embarrassed and uncertain and questioning herself.

"It has to be Rebecca. She just doesn't want to be caught," she said, her hands wringing together.

At this point, I wasn't sure what to think, other than I was tired and needed to get home. I told Charlotte I'd check in with her in the morning, and Georgie and I headed back. I did check on the Brown's door as we walked past, but it was locked up tight like I'd expected.

Still, this was all too much. I sent Uncle Chris an email

detailing what had happened during the night. I didn't want to wake him with a text but I needed to get all this out while it was still fresh. What I really needed was some more input on what exactly to do with this crazy place.

He called me the first thing in the morning. And by first thing, I mean the sky was still wearing its gray woolly sweater with nary a glimpse of light from the sun. I swear not even the birds were awake.

"Hello?" I said. At least that's what I think I said. What actually came out was something only a Wookiee could understand.

"Stella? What's this about a prowler out at the Brown house? Did you call the police?"

I tried to read the time but my eyes wouldn't focus. "It was at the house next door."

"And you went up there?"

"Uh huh." I yawned and stretched.

"Did you see them?"

"Who?"

"Stella! This is serious! The prowler."

I sat up and shook myself awake. "No, we didn't. We thought we'd have them on Charlotte's camera, but the camera got knocked down by the wind."

"So, you never saw evidence of someone actually being there?"

I knew where he was going with this and dug in my feet. "Yeah but...."

"Just the neighbor saw the prowler," he repeated.

I sighed. "Yeah."

"It could have been a branch falling that she saw. And what if it was? You raced up there. I'm surprised, honestly. Normally your head is on straight."

"My head is always straight," I replied indignantly. "And she's shown me recordings of the person before. She says it's a ghost."

"Really. You're positive that the film was unedited?"

Edited? I'd never thought of that.

Uncle Chris continued, "And what did the ghost look like?"

My cheeks filled with hot blood. "A white flicker."

There was a pause like an empty one-two drum beat. "A white flicker."

"All right. All right. You made your point," I grumbled.

"Get dressed. I'm going up there to check things out, and you're coming with me. I'll be by in thirty minutes to pick you up."

"Bring coffee," I grumbled.

And so my day started in the most cheery way.

I dressed and swept my hair in a ponytail. The muscles in my legs ached. I guess the dancing I'd done the day before had been more than I'd realized.

Uncle Chris was punctual and grim as I hobbled out of my house to meet him. He did, however, have a cup of coffee waiting for me in the holder.

Upon arriving at the Brown house he first inspected the lock and then swept it open with his card.

The door opened to darkness and that weird stale scent. His eyebrow hitched in my direction.

"I left the curtains open, I swear." I hurried over to open them.

"Maybe we should leave the slider open to air this place out."

"I'm kind of afraid to do that because the neighbor's cat was trapped in here the other day."

"Are you serious? How'd the cat get in?" he asked, following me to the door.

"There were a couple of realtor cards on the table so he must have snuck in with the buyers."

Uncle Chris stepped out on the deck. "Gorgeous!" He breathed in deeply, his chest expanding. His buttoned shirt normally would have stretched taut over his belly, but I noticed it hung loosely.

I followed him outside, still steering clear of the edge. "It really is."

"I'd have my barbecue right here and some lawn furniture. You probably couldn't get me back inside."

"They did a good job designing it. Have you ever heard any gossip that the person who built this was some kind of war criminal?"

"No, why?" he asked.

"It was something Jan from the post office mentioned. Kind of caught me off guard."

"Oh, Jan. She always makes mountains out of mole hills if she can get enough mileage out of them." He stared down the hillside. His eyes squinted and shaded his eyes from the early morning light. "What is that?"

I glanced out at the trees below me on the valley floor. The leaves were starting to change into golden tipped beauties. They rose like a living quilt, tucking in the worn mountain peaks for their winter slumber.

But, other than that, I had no idea what he was talking about.

"You see that?" Uncle Chris asked again. He pointed down the hill with his cigar. I hadn't seen him pull it out, let alone light it. "Come here." He beckoned.

Come... there? Over to that plexiglass railing that must have been put up by a sadist because who wants to be able to see straight down?

"Stella!" he called again.

I took a teeny tiny mouse step in his direction.

He pulled the cigar out of his mouth and screwed his eyes nearly shut as he stared at me. "Are you serious? You can't see it from there. Come over here."

"I'm scared of heights," I confessed. I felt my ears flush with heat. Lovely.

"Ah, I see. Well, if I can be here, you are safe." He bounced up and down with each word. Contrary to his expectations, I took a step back and grabbed for the doorframe.

"If you want me to come there, don't move," I warned.

He stuffed the cigar back in his mouth. "I won't let anything happen to you, Stella. You've got this. I promise you're safe."

"It's not a matter of being safe, it's a matter of my brain saying I'm not safe." I tiptoed out again. I don't know what tiptoeing had to do with safety, but it felt safer.

"Good job. Keep coming."

"I'm feeling brave," I lied. I crept forward. Still two feet from the railing but I could see the cavern below. It made me feel woozy. "Whoa."

"Right? What's that down there?"

He had no idea my emphatic noise had nothing to do with what he had found. I struggled to drag my gaze forward to where he was pointing.

It was yellow, like the leaves on some of the trees. What was the big deal? Had he forced me to join him to see some bush dressed in autumn colors?

I reached for his arm and held on like it was a safety-line. He grinned and put it around my shoulders. "Good job. Told you that you could do it."

"Let's not celebrate just yet. Now what do you want me to see? That thing down there?" I asked.

"Yeah, what do you think it is?"

"A shrub?"

He shook his head. "It's a bus. A school bus to be exact. I wonder why it's down there?"

"Is there a road?"

"Well, I don't think they helicoptered in, so I'm guessing that's a yes."

I ignored his sarcastic tone and instead chose to take a step back into the middle of the deck. "You think we have squatters?"

He spit over the railing. "I guess I'll have to find out."

"Well, that gives credence to Charlotte saying she's seen people here."

Uncle Chris leaned against the railing to study the house next door. My heart leapt into my throat. Surely a big man like that shouldn't be testing fate. What was that railing? Just a few flimsy nuts and bolts and—.

"You should talk to her."

"Hmm?"

"Talk to that neighbor lady and see if she's noticed the bus there before."

"Okay, fine. But can you back off the railing just a tiny bit. You're making me sweat watching you."

"How does a car racing duo like me and your dad have the same blood as you?"

"I like to race cars too," I defended hotly. "On the ground. Away from ledges."

He flicked the coal off of the cigar and stomped it with his foot. "You go talk with her. I'm going to see if there's a way down."

His words left no room for discussion. I went back into the house and sent her a text. **—Hey I'm next door right now and just saw a bus at the bottom of the property. Is that something that's been there for long?**

As I leaned against the counter I realized what was missing.

The realtor cards.

20

Every single realtor card that I'd so carefully displayed on the counter in a show of pretending there was a lot of interest had disappeared.

I shot a glance at Uncle Chris. Had he taken them?

My phone rang. "Stella, it's Charlotte. What bus are you talking about?"

"Hi, Charlotte. I'm not sure if you can see it from your house, but there's a school bus down in the valley there. Has it been there for long?"

Over the phone, I heard the sounds of a door opening and figured she was outside. After a moment, she responded. "I'm not sure. I don't think I've ever noticed it before. Then again, I rarely look in that direction."

"Okay. Weird. I kind of wondered if this might explain

where Rebecca disappears off to. Maybe she lives down there?"

She responded right away, and there was a touch of hurt in her voice. "No, I told you. She's everywhere. My bathroom, moving fruit in the fruit bowl, things like that. Plus I've seen her disappear down by the bush. You'll see. I'll get better footage. I set up the camera again, this time on my deck railing. No one will be able to knock it down there."

"But if it's a ghost, height won't stop it," I said.

"Oh..." By the uncertainty of her voice, I could tell she hadn't thought of that.

Uncle Chris wagged his finger in a circle to tell me to wrap it up.

"Well, let me know if you see her again. Okay?"

"All right."

I stared thoughtfully at my phone after we hung up. I still didn't know what to think.

"I'm heading down to the bus. You coming?" he asked.

"Uh...." I didn't get a chance to answer. He was already out the front door, probably assuming I was following him.

By the time I got outside, Uncle Chris was nowhere in sight.

"Over here," Uncle Chris called from behind the house. I met up with him near the hedge to see a rough-hewn, rock stairwell. "You ready for a work out?"

My leg was stabilized in the boot, but I definitely didn't want to overdo it. "How many are there?"

He traveled down about five where they disappeared behind a thick row of blackberry bushes. "There's a bunch, but the steps are well made. I think you can do it. I'll help you if you need it."

There was a handrail made of a thin tree stripped of its bark. Carefully, I picked my way down the stairs.

At the bottom, the undergrowth of shrubs, wild grass, and saplings was thick and taller than my head. I reached Uncle Chris, feeling a little breathless and sticky from anxiety sweat.

He pulled his cigar stub from his pocket and relit it. Gray clouds puffed up as he squinted his eyes. "Someone's been down here recently."

"How can you tell?" I stepped forward to see what he was seeing, only to get snagged by a blackberry branch for my efforts.

"Exactly." He leveled the cigar at another branch where a piece of cloth fluttered. "Someone got hung up on these on the way down. Or up." He glanced back at the house. The only thing we could see from here was the underside of the top deck.

"Come on. Let's keep going and find out where this trail leads, hmm?"

He clenched the cigar between his teeth like it was a stick of pepperoni and headed off with mountainous steps. The ground was thick with fallen leaves, but luckily, not slick. I followed after him and tried to keep a sharp eye out for spider webs. The last thing I needed was some Kung Fu flailing action scene that ended with my shirt being ripped off as I tumbled down the hillside.

We walked a few minutes.

I broke the silence. "Hey, I meant to ask you. Did you happen to grab the realtor business cards from the counter?"

"Why would I do that?"

"I have no idea, but they're missing."

His forehead wrinkled. "Weird. Maybe another realtor swiped them because they want us to think there isn't any interest."

Now that we were down here and moving, I could see a trail. Places where the leaves had been kicked back and the grass worn down to bare dirt.

Who had been down here? Mr. Brown? Was this where he'd been shot?

"You think this is a deer trail?" I asked as we skirted around a large tree. He paused at the bottom of a boulder and held his hand out to help me over it.

"Don't think so." He spoke around the cigar still clenched between his teeth.

"Why not?"

"The deer around here leave thinner trails. Not to mention the grass is usually pushed to the side, not destroyed like it is here.

We descended deeper into the trees. I glanced over my shoulder, but the house had disappeared behind a dense interwoven screen of branches. The thought that someone could travel down here unseen was spooky.

"You think this was made by people then?" I grabbed a branch to steady myself.

He grunted in reply.

"Like maybe hunters?" It made sense. Mr. Brown was killed by a rifle shot.

"No. Not hunters."

"Why not?"

He paused and removed the cigar. "Because hunters try not to leave a scent trail behind. You beat a trail into the ground like this, there's a scent miles wide."

I frowned. "Would any hunter know that?"

"Most experienced ones, yeah."

"Because you know how Mr. Brown died."

"Yeah. Yeah. I know." The cigar resumed its place, and he continued forward.

A few minutes later the trail flattened, and I realized we'd reached the bottom. I chanced another look toward the house, and then froze, realizing I had a clear shot of the sliding glass door. Anyone sitting here could see what was going on inside the house. I tried to see Charlotte's house, but that was still hidden by trees.

"Uncle Chris. Look." I pointed up to the Brown house.

His eyebrows rose in surprise and he exhaled deeply, his nostrils flaring. "Someone down here could have quite a show, hmm?" he finally said.

"Scary. And the people inside would never know."

"With the right binoculars, you could see someone programing the microwave for some popcorn."

Or maybe punching in a safe combination, I thought. The hair at the base of my scalp rose at the thought. I rubbed my neck and shivered.

"Alright, keep going. Almost there," he said, turning back.

We stepped over a shallow rivulet of water, and I wondered if this came from the white pipes that the RandCo builder had mentioned a while back. The mud squelched under our shoes and crept up the sides. I frowned at my boot as the mud got under my toes. I closed my eyes and reminded myself it was coming off next week and tried to pick my way to drier ground.

That ground proved to be a pine needle carpet that reminded me of beetles and tiny mushrooms, adding to the loamy scent rising from the forest floor. Conifers blocked most of the sunlight.

We finally navigated behind the last rhododendron hedge and before us lay the object of our hike.

The school bus.

The bus was old. It was easy to conclude that fact, and not just because the windows were scuzzed out with moss and algae. It had an antique curved front, round headlights and a weird back. Someone had brought it here years ago.

Slowly, we approached it, with me trailing behind Uncle

Chris. He furtively searched the ground, while I followed, still worried about my boot.

It was then I saw the foot prints.

It was a boot print, rather big, but mostly hidden under a fallen leaf. I might have missed it if I didn't look right then. Pointed toe, with a slight heel, it looked to be a cowboy or hiking boot.

"Hey, Uncle Chris!" I called.

"What did you find?" he asked, walking over. As he stood next to me, I knew for sure he was losing weight. But another thing stood out to me. He didn't have the beads of sweat popping out on his forehead that he normally did.

"Uncle Chris... you look good," I said with an approving grin.

His lip quivered around the clenched cigar with a hint of a smile. Then he nodded and puffed on the stogie. "Thanks, Stella." A cloud of smoke hid his serious gaze as he squatted to see the print. He used a stick to flip the leaf off.

"You think it could be that neighbor lady poking around here?

I shook my head. "She's pretty tiny. I'm sure her feet are smaller than mine. Besides, she has a limp. I have high doubts she could get down the hill."

I maneuvered my good foot next to it for size and snapped a picture.

"Good find. Let's keep looking."

We wandered around to the door of the bus. I was stunned to see a rusty chain and hooks laying on the ground.

Uncle Chris noted them as well. "Choker chain and some cable. Old logging equipment. Interesting. Maybe this was once a logging camp."

He pulled out a handkerchief from his pocket, and used it to grip the handle. The door stuck. Grunting, he shimmied it open.

It screeched back, revealing a long drapey spider web. I saw it and shivered. Uncle Chris didn't see it. Instead, he stabbed the chewed on cigar in the direction of the iron plated metal steps. It took everything I had to drag my eyes away, but I saw what had him so interested.

There were muddy footprints across the steps.

"You ready?" He squinted at me.

I shook my head. There was no way I was going into that spider infested cavern. I bet those arachnids were watching me now, with all twenty eyes—or whatever number they had —just zeroed in on my pink vulnerable skin. The roof was probably covered in cobwebs. I bet the bugs would just rain down.

My head shakes were violent now. "N-no way. There are spiders in there."

Uncle Chris rolled his eyes so hard, I thought he'd hurt himself. "Are you being serious right now? A brave strong woman like yourself? Afraid of spiders?"

"Even Superman had kryptonite."

"Ahh," he said. "But you aren't Superman. You are Superwoman, and we all know who was stronger."

There it was, the gauntlet thrown down. Was I going to accept it?

"Come on. I believe in you." With that, he gripped the metal handrail and slowly eased onto the bus. The bus sagged on its wheels under his weight, which, even though it seemed to be less, was still considerable.

He ducked his head under the web and disappeared down the aisle. I licked my bottom lip, now dry and chapped. *Okay, girl. This is it. Do you really want to walk away and know a bus beat you?*

I reached for the handrail and took the first step. Something tickled my neck, and I squealed. It was a pine needle, dropped from the pile sitting on the edge of the door.

"Stella! Check this out!" Uncle Chris called.

I eyed the wobbling cobweb above me. Ducking and eyeing, I somehow managed to squirm under it while dragging a clunky boot. I found myself standing where the driver's seat once was, feeling more skittish than a horse in a cloud of blood-thirsty flies.

"What do you think?" Uncle Chris squatted in front of a little wood stove. He had the door open and was shining the flashlight from his phone inside. There were chunks of firewood stacked to the side, waiting to be fed into the round iron belly. A pipe shot up at several angles until it pierced the roof and was covered with streaks of rust from the leaking rain.

All the seats had been removed. In their place was some sort of a bed, covered with dirty blankets and a few scattered granola bar wrappers. It made me shudder just trying to imagining sleeping there. Who knew what crept over you in your sleep.

At the head of the bed (at least, I thought it was the head. There was no pillow to speak of) was something glittering. I made a quick glance for anything crawling around and then bent to pick it up.

"What's this?" I asked, holding the silicon blob. I turned it over in my fingers, my brain almost recognizing it.

Uncle Chris glanced over my shoulder. "That's a piece from a pair of eye glasses. You know, one of those nose pads?"

Oh, yeah. I could see it now. The thing that sat on the bridge of the nose. Often made dents in the skin.

He leaned to peer through the moisture covered windows. "Yeah. I think probably the bus came from an old logging company years ago. Since then, the trees have closed in on the road it came in on. As to who's been here now, I've got no clue. But someone was here recently. The ashes in this stove are still fresh. They haven't hardened like they would after years of being here."

We poked around for a few minutes more. Uncle Chris casually pointed out a roach that watched us from the metal side of the bus. It seemed to notice the attention because it scurried up the wall to disappear under the metal trim of the window.

My heebie-jeebies were off the chart. I batted around my head at imagined spiders and bugs. A drip of water on the back of my ear about made me lose my mind. I couldn't handle it any more. I had to get out of here.

Uncle Chris laughed as I scrambled along the aisle and down the stairs. He followed after me.

"You did good," he said. "That was pretty gross in there."

"Thanks," I breathed in the sweet outdoor air. Nothing was going to convince me to go back in there. Disgusting.

We were nearing the rhododendrons again when I saw something else. Something that made me stop dead in my tracks.

21

A soda can, with its silver end, poked out of the undergrowth. It was the same brand as the one I'd nearly tripped over my first day here. I reached with a stick and spun it out. From the keyhole mouth spilled cigarette butts.

"Look at this!" I gasped.

Chris nudged the can with his foot. "Interesting."

"What's interesting is that I found the same can with a cigarette in it up at the house. You don't suppose Mr. Brown smoked?"

He shook his head. "If he did, it was only outside. There's not a trace of the scent inside."

"And Charlotte had never seen him before. I find that pretty unlikely if he was a smoker. It must be someone else, then." I snapped a shot of the can with my phone.

I couldn't rule out Mr. Brown, yet. Charlotte had said Mr. Brown had his groceries delivered. Maybe I could find out if he bought cigarettes.

We headed back to the house. This time, Uncle Chris offered his hand to help me over the creek and around a fallen log. His cigar was out, but he was still chomping on it. I could tell something was on his mind.

I thought about asking, but I wasn't sure if hiking back up a hill while trying to breathe was the right time to broach important questions. Then again, maybe it would be easier for him, since he wasn't facing me.

"So, how are things going with Oscar?" The question blurted from my mouth before I was done processing if I wanted to ask it or not. I had to admit, the filter between my thoughts and mouth was not strong.

He snorted. "It's like you read my mind."

"Really!" I said, surprised. I grabbed a low branch to help pull me up. "What's going on?"

"There's something I've been meaning to tell you," he mumbled.

I shot him a fierce look that, if he had seen it, could hardly fail to convey the spike in my anxiety. Talk about famous last words! He'd used that exact phrase with me months ago to start the whole discussion about my mother. What was he going to say now? I couldn't take it, I really couldn't. Why had I even started this?

"I—uh— I've been seeing a therapist."

I paused so fast I actually slid backward on the hill from the lack of momentum.

He heard the crunching leaves and turned quickly with a concerned look. "You okay?"

Pull it together, Stella. He's sharing his heart here. "Yeah. I'm fine. Wow. So, how's that going?"

He patted his pocket where he kept his cigars, despite the fact that there was one still clenched between his teeth. A sure sign that he was extra nervous. He seemed to realize and pulled the wet nub from his mouth and gave it a critical inspection. "It's going okay. She's actually really helping me." He cleared his throat, and I was surprised to see a flush creep over the top of his shirt collar. "I discovered something about myself. I've been punishing myself for years. You know, for what happened with your mom. I think, somewhere in my pin head, I'd decided that if I gained weight, I would avoid ever having a relationship. I thought I didn't deserve one, after what I did to your family." He stared down sadly.

"Oh, Uncle Chris," I breathed, suddenly choked up.

"I'm working through it. Trying to get my head healthy."

"I guess it's having an effect on your physical health as well."

"Yeah," he laughed and smacked his stomach. "It really has. Amazing."

"We need to take you shopping maybe. Your clothes aren't fitting very well." I limped closer and gave him a hug.

"I'm so proud of you. I know how hard that must have been, facing your fears like that and sharing with someone."

"It was hard. But then I figured I'm paying for it, and I sure as heck wasn't going to waste that money."

I laughed. Trust penny-pinching to come to the rescue.

We'd just reached the top of the hill when my phone rang. It was the lawyer. I put him on speaker and gestured to Uncle Chris. His eyebrows rose in interest as he read the caller's name.

"Stella, It's Clarence Brighton. I wanted to give you an update. Derek Armstrong is off the board that will be deciding your mother's parole. He knows he's under investigation for covering up his daughter's murder. When your mother gets out, it will be up to her to see if she wants another court case, unless, in a stroke of good luck, we can get Clegg to confess. And we might be able to do that."

Clegg was the man who worked for Armstrong. He was also the one that ran me off the road, causing my broken leg. "How so?"

"It's possible the prosecutor might offer him leniency if he flips on Derek."

I swallowed hard, not at all sure I wanted leniency for someone who'd tried to kill me and very nearly succeeded. It was all too soon. I was still in a boot, for crying out loud.

"What are they going to offer him? Like amnesty?"

"No. Nothing like that. Clegg will be getting locked up for a long time. However, it's a difference if he spends his time at

Ashmount Penitentiary or a cushier one. And he has the possible chance of parole in fifteen years."

My grip relaxed on the phone. "And you think for sure he will be convicted?"

"Your car's paint is all over his grill. He's on camera following you. The tire marks match his tires. He's going away. We just need to use what we can for the good of your mother."

My mom had been locked away for twenty years for a murder she hadn't committed. One that Clegg himself had done.

"But, barring a confession from Clegg, we do have an ace in the hole."

"What's that?"

"I've hired a private investigator who located two of the gang members that were there the day your mother was arrested. Since then, they've both left the crime lifestyle and moved away. One has become a physician's assistant, and the other is a manager at a hotel. Looks like they're both willing to point the finger at Clegg. So, with their testimony, I don't think it will take much to convince Clegg to roll over on Armstrong."

"That's amazing." I smiled.

"Either way, your mom is getting out next week. In the meantime, keep those fingers crossed, pray, or do whatever you do to keep positive."

"Got it. Thank you so much."

I hung up, and Uncle Chris and I stared at each other like two owls.

"Next week. What do you think about that?" he asked.

"I'm numb."

"Numb?"

I considered for a second and shook my head. "No, really I feel like my emotions are a deck of cards caught in a never-ending shuffle. But I don't feel in a rush to figure things out. For the first time, I feel comfortable with letting things stay messy and giving it time to sort itself out."

He clapped my shoulder and squeezed. "That's a good place to be."

———

22

Even as Uncle Chris drove me home, those emotional cards still were fluttering. There was so much out of my control, and it was driving me crazy.

Not to mention all these weird bits and pieces of the Brown house competing for head space. What was going on there? Who'd been staying in that bus?

When Uncle Chris dropped me off at the top of my driveway, I was immediately felt flooded with that warm, welcome-home feeling. Walking inside was like getting a hug. My house was safe, shockingly clean, and smelled like the cinnamon reeds I'd placed about. I dropped my jacket and purse off on the side table and headed to the kitchen for some coffee and a snack.

While the coffee brewed, I opened the fridge to consider

my options. Let's see, leftover pizza? Soup? Maybe that salad back there?

My gaze landed on a piece of apple pie from the other night. How I managed to still have it, I'll never know. I eagerly ripped off the plastic wrap before sticking it in the microwave.

A minute later found me curled up in my favorite easy chair by the window, coffee mug and phone sitting in the window sill. I balanced my plate and laptop on my lap like an expert and took a syrupy apple bite. Mmmm.

It was time to do some research.

First, I searched for local grocery stores in the town of Gainesville looking for ones that delivered.

I found one nearby. Taking a swig of coffee to wash down the pie, I dialed their number. My nose wrinkled as an automated voice answered. It took a minute to navigate through their options, but I finally was on hold for a manager.

"Glenda speaking, how can I help you?"

"Hi, there. My name is Stella, and I'm a realtor. I'm calling you in regards to a client of mine."

"Okay?" Uncertainty colored her voice.

"His name was David Brown, and he ordered all of his groceries exclusively to be delivered. I was wondering if you knew if he was a customer of yours."

"Oh, sure. Up on Reeter's Ridge? He's been with us for a

long time. I was so shocked and saddened to hear what happened."

"I know. It was a tragedy. There are some questions actually that have come up, and I'm just trying to gather all the information I can about him. He was a recluse, you know."

"Yes, we did assume that. How can I help you?"

"I was curious if he was a big soda drinker or if he purchased cigarettes?"

"Oh!" She was curious now, I could tell. "Give me one moment. We have old orders on file for inventory." I heard typing, along with an intercom going off in the background announcing the daily special. After a moment, she said, "No, no I don't see anything here like that. No sodas, no cigarettes. Does that help?"

Wow, so it had been someone else. "Thank you. That's what we suspected, but it's nice to have it confirmed." Then something prompted me to ask, "Was there anything unusual about his orders?"

I was surprised when she hummed a "Mmhmm."

Tingles spiked up my spine. What was I about to learn?

"He purchased quite a bit of bulk dried items."

"Really? What is that exactly?"

"Commercial-sized bags of rice, beans, flour, and freeze dried food. Nearly every order had some components of those."

"Wow!" And then I cringed at giving away my excitement.

I tried to sound more professional. "Thank you so much. I'm sure that will really help."

"You're welcome! Just let me know if there's anything else I can do."

I hung up and took another bite of apple pie, deep in thought. Something was coming to me.

The original Browns had hired an out-of-town company to draw up the plans. The contractor I'd talked with mentioned there was something odd about the foundations. He'd also made another comment, one I'd shrugged to one side. That the white pipes weren't just for water drainage, but were for ventilation.

Air.

Now, Glenda's info made the groceries sound an awful lot like bunker food. Was there a weird bunker under the house?

Did that have anything to do with his death? Had there been someone watching him from the school bus below, and shot him when Mr. Brown came outside?

But why?

I searched up Century Bank again, hoping to find the banner with the woman in it who had come to the house showing. It was a long shot, but that's what this all was.

Finally, I located it and clicked the ad. A page flashed on the screen with her smiling face, along with a photo of a family and kids having fun, a dog shaking off water in a sprinkler, and lots of headlines telling me how safe my money would be with them.

I scrolled to the bottom of the page to the tiny letters that said "web master" and clicked it. I was brought to a page that asked me if I was having trouble viewing the original link.

In the space provided, I asked if there was any way I could contact the people in the bank's banner. It was a weird question, and all I could do was cross my fingers and hope for the best.

Sipping my coffee, my thoughts went back to the first potential buyer I'd shown the house to, and when I saw him later at the ax throwing competition.

Greasy-haired Gary. He'd seemed awful shifty when he came through the house. As well as flirty. My skin crawled, thinking of his leer. That'd been a good time to test out my pepper spray. Right in the eyes. KaPow! What were you looking at again?

And that's the moment you get arrested for assault, my inner voice chimed in. As usual, it was ruining all the fun.

Still, I wondered if I could find anything about him. Didn't Frank say he worked at Century Bank during the time of the safety deposit theft? Chills crawled up my arms as I remembered he wore glasses as well. Maybe he was missing a nose piece, hmm? I typed in Studebaker, and Century Bank and hit enter.

Amazingly enough, his picture came up. Apparently, he was still a manager at the bank, dressed slightly nicer in a sweater, but with the same slicked back comb-over and thick-framed glasses.

If he worked there when Mr. Brown was the auditor, was it possible they collaborated? Maybe Mr. Brown kept all the stolen items and never gave Gary his share. Maybe that's what Gary was searching for while he was there.

But the house was as empty as could be. Did the moving company take them when the trustee ordered the house packed? Or was this proof there was some sort of hidden hole or room?

I thought about Sam Smith, and his girlfriend, Miss NoName. Hadn't they brought up the idea of picking off the fireplace bricks? Surely there wouldn't be any space big enough back there to store what was missing.

What was stolen again? I dug around a bit to find the list of missing items. It wasn't complete by far, but some things on it were World War Two medals, coins, a load of watches including a 6B/159 navigator watch. Several pistols, one being the Walther P38. Among the rarest was a priceless journal of Winston Churchill's in which he penned his speeches.

Not one of those things had turned up again.

A hunch made me search up the name of the watch. The answer came up, and I stared at it, stunned. The watch dated from WWII. I next searched up the pistol which told me it was German, also from that time period.

All of these items were war memorabilia or from that decade.

Noise from outside slowly broke my concentration. I

glanced through the window. The birds were going crazy, swooping and dive bombing the ground.

What in the world? I leaned forward to watch, then suddenly spotted the neighbor's cat. Mr. Gato crouched with slitted eyes and a wiggling bottom in the air. His tail lashed as he prepared to spring.

I didn't need to know what he was looking at. I knew I had to stop him. I tried to sit up, feeling like a floundering seal, before finally getting my feet on the ground. Boot pounding, I hurried to the door and flung it open.

"Mr. Gato!" I yelled. I actually had no idea what the cat's name really was. It's just what I called him.

I needn't have worried. One of the birds flew down and buzzed the cat's head. The cat stared around with wild eyes. Another bird took up where the first one left and flew at the animal. Mr. Gato had enough and sprinted away, ears flattened.

Crazy cat. What was he after? Squinting, I saw what had his focus. A baby bird on the ground. There was a nest in the fork of the branch above him.

I rushed over and then chewed my thumbnail, wondering what to do. If I put him back in the nest, would the mother bird reject him? I couldn't very well leave him down here for the cat to come back for a little snack.

I scooped him up gently and placed him in the little grass cup. I suppose I'd have to check later and see how the parents did. Surprisingly, I thought it was going to be okay. They seemed to settle down as I headed back into the house.

When I came back to my chair I saw my email was answered by the web master. They suggested that I check with the local talent agency.

Local talent agency... okay. I started to hunt for the agency when another idea came to me. I went to the original banner and took a screen shot of her face. Then I slipped into the search engine under reverse photo search.

Can I just say there are moments when I feel brilliant? No, not when I accidentally drop my phone in the toilet, or the time I lost my earring in the garbage disposal. But this moment right here, this was one of them.

The reverse photo search brought up a social media page. The woman had shared a copy of the commercial banner to her friends, maybe to brag. I couldn't see her full profile. It was set to private.

But I did have a name.

23

J ennifer Barker. Now we were getting somewhere. Her page told me who her boyfriend was by linking it to his relationship status on social media. A Mr. Sam Smith. No surprise there.

It also linked to her current employment. She worked as a receptionist at the local Lasik doctor. I nodded to myself, remembering Georgie mention some smart-aleck comment Sam had made when he met her. That could be how Sam and Jennifer met.

I was on to something... I knew I was. Did Jennifer know Gary Studebaker? Had she met him while she modeled for the bank's banner?

My phone rang, scaring me half to death. I answered it once I saw it was Georgie.

"Hey, Stella. I have to tell you I've been poking around a

little bit," Georgie's sentences flew out like she was sprinting with her words.

"Poking around, how?" I asked, cautiously.

"I told Cecelia that you were representing the Brown house, and she had all sorts of questions. Like you suspected, the people who built the house were really weird."

"What did she want to know?"

"Mainly about Mr. Brown's sister, Alice."

"Oh. She died a while back. The trustee sold the place to Charlotte."

"Are you sure she died? Cecelia seemed to think there was some kind of controversy on that."

I frowned. "What's the controversy about her death?"

"I guess because she died out of state."

"She did? What state?"

"Cecelia heard Florida."

I typed in the trustee's name who'd sold both houses. Mr. Coleman was also located in Florida, in the same town that the original Mrs. Brown lived in the nursing home facility.

"Have you talked with Carlson lately?" Georgie abruptly asked.

My mental detective gears screeched to a halt. "Uh, what?"

"Carlson. Have you kept him up to speed with all this weirdness?"

"No," I admitted. I hadn't talked to him again since he mentioned his date. My heart couldn't take it.

"You should. Honestly, I've never seen him so happy in a long long time. He's always has this huge wall up and never lets anyone in."

Little did she know that with each word she was heaping coals on my head. This was crushing. Who was this new girl he was seeing? I wanted to tear her apart. What was this, jealousy?

Yes. Intense jealousy, regret, and so much pain.

"I have to go," I said, trying to hide how that comment flared my emotions. We hung up, and I looked at my coffee. I felt like I needed something stronger than that right now.

I rubbed my head trying to cope, trying to deal. Sometimes I really hated emotions. Sometimes, I wished I really was numb. I took a deep breath, and realized I might be unpacking emotions about Carlson for a while. But I needed to get back into good headspace. I needed to be strong for me.

So, pushing Carlson into a wrinkled corner of that cerebellum of mine, I grabbed a notebook and wrote down the names, Gary Studebaker, Sam Smith, and Jennifer Barker. I chewed a thumbnail, staring at the last name. Why was it tugging on a memory?

I jolted. I knew where I'd heard the name, the last name anyway. Miss Dolly had said that there was a boy named Tommy Barker who had a crush on Alice Brown. He'd pulled her hair. I remember now. I typed his name into social media, wondering how anyone did any detective stuff before the web.

There were a couple profiles that popped up. I clicked the first that wasn't private.

"I'm just going to put my snoopy de snoop snoop hat on and take a peek," I whispered, carefully perusing the man's pictures. Being extra careful, actually. I could just see myself accidentally liking one of them.

Bingo! I giggled at what I found. The man was married and had a full family. A family that was tagged with names at what appeared to be a barbecue. And one of those names was a certain Jennifer Barker. Sam Smith appeared by her side, lifting a beer bottle with a cigarette in his hand.

I plugged Gary Studebaker's name into the social media site. Was there a link between Jennifer and him?

A Gary Studebaker popped up—just one—but still I wasn't sure if it was him. The profile picture was of some type of patch. I zoomed to see it better. It was a blue circle with a pouncing winged tiger. On the top was a white star with a red circle in the center. I'd never seen anything like it.

Hoping search images would give me something once again, I copied it and pasted the picture in the search bar. Moments later it found a match.

My jaw dropped so far, I could have caught a humming bird. The picture was identified as a WWII Army Air Corps 14th Air Force Class patch.

World War II. I couldn't believe I was seeing it again. Was

this the same Gary that worked at Century Bank? If it was, it couldn't be his patch. He wasn't that old. Did he have the same fascination with war memorabilia as David apparently did?

Maybe I should give Carlson a call. Did I dare?

But he's so happy. Can I handle hearing how happy he is with someone else?

I again was caught with how differently this felt compared to Richie and his date. I was happy for Richie.

I was *not* happy about Carlson. And I wasn't sure if I was strong enough to fake it.

But I missed him. I really did. And I had news. Maybe he could help. Maybe just a text. What could it hurt? I could fake anything over a text message.

I decided to do it. **—Hey. Have a second to talk?**

I set the phone on the table and picked up my mug. Taking a sip, I stared out the window at the nest. The ice-cold coffee jolted me alert, and I nearly spit it back in the cup.

But I swallowed it instead with a smile. Momma bird perched on the edge of the nest with a worm. My heart swelled in relief.

The good feelings were dashed when my phone rang, and I saw it was Carlson. What? He was calling? He hated talking on the phone!

My vocal cords felt tight as I answered, "Hi, Carlson. I didn't expect you to call." I got up and walked to the porch to pace, nervous.

"I figured I should. Been a while since I've heard from you. What's up?"

I forced myself to sound casual. "So, how was your date?"

"Date? Oh! Yeah, the date."

"Did you have fun?"

"Yeah, yeah." He impatiently plowed forward. "Is that why I haven't heard from you lately?"

"Well, I've been busy," I said. "Trying to sell that house up on Reeter's Ridge. I think the guy was murdered. In fact, I'm sure of it."

He snorted. "Couldn't happen to a more deserving fellow."

"Can I ask you something? Did the stuff that disappeared from your grandfather's security box have to do with World War II?"

"That's a weird question, but yeah. His memorabilia and some stocks from back then. Why do you ask?"

"It seems to be a theme." I sat on the porch swing and set it moving with a toe. "You think it could still be hidden there?"

"Where?"

"At the Brown house. I'm starting to wonder if there's some type of hidden room. Like a walled-up closet or bunker or something. I think he was killed for either the theft or the actually stolen stuff itself. And get this, there's a bus at the bottom of the property. Anyone down there had a perfect view of the interior of the house. I found soda cans and cigarette butts both down there and in the driveway."

"Interesting. Of course, I always had my doubts about it being an accidental gun shot from the beginning. That shot was too clean."

"Clean, how? Like they were aiming?"

"Yeah. Straight to the heart."

Well, that was a disturbing visual. "Why were they so quick to rule it a hunting accident?"

"I'm not a part of the Brookfield police department. That'd be a question you should ask them."

"I think this guy, Gary Studebaker, is the main suspect."

"Really? I can't wait to hear how you came to that deduction."

Snarky as always. "It makes sense. He worked at the bank when this all happened. He came to the house under the guise of a buyer and started snooping around, like he knew what he was looking for. And get this, he has WWII memorabilia as his picture on his Facebook."

I didn't hear any response. "Carlson?"

"I'm listening. Hollywood, when will you figure out that life isn't a movie? You're pinning this on him because of a Facebook picture? I don't know a lot but I know the police force in Gainesville aren't stupid. They had that guy under a microscope, and he came up clean."

The insult stung. I bit off my response that wanted to lash back.

"Listen, you want to talk more about this?" he asked.

"I've got to go," I said, frustrated. That date of his could have him.

My inner voice was calling me a liar before I even finished ending the call.

24

Okay, I couldn't fix my situation with Carlson, but I could try to figure this mystery out. He really seemed convinced Gary was innocent. If Gary was innocent, then who was the key to all of this? The more that I dug into this, the more confused I was.

That house was definitely unlucky. All the relatives who'd owned it had died, with the exception of David Brown's mom in the nursing home.

Then there was that weird apparition, Rebecca. Thinking about her reminded me I'd been meaning to see if there'd been anything that had happened in Charlotte's house to a woman.

I did a cursory search to see if there'd been any crimes. The only thing that came up was Mr. Brown's death and Charlotte's many phone calls for prowlers.

I remembered how Charlotte had said she'd never seen the car that the prowler had left in. Was it possible it was because he was slipping down the hill and staying in the bus?

I put a phone call in to the Trustee's office. I needed to know more about Alice's death.

"How is the sale going?" Mr. Coleman asked me when I was finally patched through.

"It's going okay. I had a few questions about the house next door. I found out you sold it a few years ago."

"Yes, that's right."

"Did her death certificate show where she died?"

"What do you mean?"

"Well it was Alice Brown's. And you sold it when she died?"

"We don't know anything about that. We sold it on request of Mr. David Brown himself. He owned both houses."

"He owned both houses? I thought one was owned by Alice?"

"No. It seems when the elder Mr. Brown died, he left both the houses to his son. The first house was sold just over two years ago last spring."

We hung up and I rubbed my neck. Wait, when had the house sold? Two years ago? Right when the safety deposit box theft happened. I knew Charlotte had lived there for two years, but the coincidence in the dates hadn't occurred to me before now.

I'd wondered how Mr. Brown had been able to afford to live without a job. Now I had a clue as to how. He was living off the house proceeds. They brought in quite a pretty penny, I was sure.

But why had he done it? On the one hand, it was obvious, who wouldn't want to quit work and start retirement as soon as possible? Still, he'd turned into a recluse and had never left. What was his motive?

I thought about the weird things that had happened up until now. The missing realtor cards from the counter. The lock box sabotaged, and the unique foundation the builder had mentioned. The conversations I'd heard from Sam and Jennifer, and the way both they and Gary Studebaker snooped around. That open house was a disaster.

Then there were the signs of someone living in the school bus and the prowler Charlotte saw. The missing key from the desk. The cat that was locked in the room, and the curtains always being closed. Cigarettes, soda cans, footprints, and eyeglass pieces. It seemed like a never-ending list of strange things.

One thing stood out in my mind. People were certain that Mr. Brown was behind the theft of the safety deposit boxes, and they seemed certain that the contents of the boxes were hidden in the house.

There had to be a hidden room, some hideyhole or whatever. I had to go back. Maybe that's what the white pipes connected to at the bottom of the property. I'd just walk around the place and see if I saw an outside entrance. Decision made, I grabbed my pepper spray and headed to my car.

The entire trip to Gainesville, I had an internal argument with myself. Now, a normal person would be arguing over the wisdom of checking out the Brown house unaccompanied. But that was a nonissue for me. After all, I represented the house. As a realtor I had to be used to being alone in houses all the time.

No, the argument I was having was over Carlson. Unlike Richie, I had the sinking feeling that I would not be able to remain friends with him if he was in a relationship. I beat myself up for being so dumb as to not let him know I was interested in him earlier. I know he would have gone for it. Why had I waited? Now I'd lost the one person I'd truly cared about in a long time. My heart felt like it weighed more than the boot on my foot.

I hated emotions.

I drove up Reeter's Ridge and turned down the Brown driveway. The flyer box by the road was empty, so I grabbed more flyers and stuffed it full. Then I headed to the house. The yard was a mess with colorful piles of leaves and scattered branches. I needed to get the gardener back out here.

I froze just as the porch came into view.

The front door was open.

I swallowed hard and called Charlotte. She answered with her usual chipper hello.

I came straight to the point. "Charlotte, have you seen anyone at the Brown house recently?"

"Well, there was a house showing this morning. And it's been a windy day!"

I nodded. That could explain it. Maybe the door stuck, and the wind blew it open. After all, there were signs of a windstorm everywhere.

"I have a strange favor to ask," I said, stepping out of the car. I peeked into the interior of the house. Just like last time, the darn curtains were closed.

"What is it?"

"The door was open, so I'm going to do a quick search. If you don't hear from me in ten minutes, would you call the police?"

Her breath caught on the other end. "Are you okay?"

"Yeah, I'm sure everything's fine. I just want to have a back-up in the one in a million chance it isn't."

"Okay, you got it. Setting my alarm now!"

We hung up, and I checked the time. Ten minutes wasn't very long, and I realized I needed to get a move on. I walked inside and was immediately accosted by the strong scent of perfume. The realtor and buyers must not have left that long ago. I set my purse on the counter. Grabbing my pepper spray, I headed to the bedrooms.

It was a spooky search. So far, everything seemed to be in place.

I stood in front of the staircase for a good moment, trying to muster the courage to check the basement. I hated it down there. Finally, I took the steps, reminding myself over and over that Charlotte would call the police if she didn't hear from me.

The main room was empty. I checked the bathroom and then flung open the door to the bonus room.

Empty.

Relieved, I called Charlotte. "Everything is fine, no need to send in the cavalry."

"Thank goodness! I tell you my heart was pounding. I saw Rebecca again last night. She seemed more frantic than usual."

"Why didn't you call?"

"She disappeared after only a few moments. I watched for her to return but she never did."

Distracted, I thanked her again and hung up. Something had caught my attention. It was nothing much, and I might have ignored it, had Charlotte not amped my anxiety with the comment about Rebecca's return.

It was a leaf. One single golden leaf similar to the millions that lay in colorful mounds outside. It lay right next to the wall.

I walked over and looked at it. It had a wet impression, like it had been dragged in by someone's heel. Its position on the floor made it appear as though the person who'd scraped it off had disappeared right through the wall.

Lightly, I touched the wall. I moved the chair and leaned my ear against it to listen. The surface was cool to my cheek, and I could only hear my own pulse pounding.

I ran my fingers over the paint and searched for any irregularity or divot. There was nothing. I turned to the next wall and did the same, and then the next.

Nothing.

I took a bold step and started knocking on the drywall. In every instance the walls proved to be solid.

I sank to the floor in a puddle of disappointment and rested my head against the wall. *What did I expect? Some secret entrance to a bunker gone wild? My imagination did it again. Maybe Carlson was right. I did expect everything to end up like a movie.*

My disappointment cut so thick I might have actually shed a tear or two. What stopped me was that darn leaf, again. I scooted over to examine it one more time. It really did look like it had been scraped off by accident while mysteriously leaving the room.

It was then I noticed the corner of the carpet. A smudge in one spot, above the leaf. It was so faint, I never would have noticed it while standing. I reached for the smudge, matched my fingers over it and saw they coincided. I plucked at the carpet.

The entire corner lifted up to reveal a trap door.

Excitement charged me. With feverish energy I swung it back.

Stairs led down to a brightly lit room. Sitting in a chair at the bottom, as though waiting for me, was a thin woman dressed in white.

25

"Hello," she said, seemingly uncaring to my barging in to her hidey-hole. She was equally oblivious to my eyes as round as sausage patties as I peered down.

"H-hi," I mustered back.

"Your leg, how is it?" The woman's gray hair was piled into a chignon at the base of her neck. Her shoes, something about her shoes was incredibly off. I stared hard trying to figure it out. All I came away with was that they looked to be too small for the footprints I'd found down by the bus.

She watched me like I was a curiosity, a fuzzy caterpillar or a turtle. Her face showed no signs of surprise.

My gaze flicked around the room. The air held a tinge of mustiness, the same scent I'd picked up every time I'd entered the house. From what I could see the walls were cement and lined with bolted shelves filled with every type of sundry goods and boxes you could imagine. I saw the previously mentioned bags of flour and beans, along with cases of bottled water.

"What is this place?" I whispered.

"Papa called it our secret room. Would you like to see more?" She spoke as softly as one could without whispering. It was the voice of someone who moved in silence.

"Maybe in a minute." I took a breath and swallowed, trying to regroup. I glanced at her shoes again, realizing what was wrong. I'd never seen anything like them before. Leather and with thick heels, festooned with giant leather bows across the arch. They looked like antiques.

I realized I gripped the can of pepper spray like it was a grenade I was about to launch. Slowly, I loosened my hand, feeling cramps throughout my fingers. "Alice, is that you?"

"Oh." The woman smiled, appearing quite pleased. "You know me, then."

"I do," I said. "But the rumor is that you passed away in Florida. Did you know that?"

She ducked her head. "David did that. He wanted to sell the place and thought that would be the cleanest way. After all, it agreed with our ultimate plan."

"Which was?"

"To live here, of course. Under the house."

"Why would you do that?"

"Papa always said the end was coming. We needed to be

prepared and we needed to protect our history. He spent his lifetime doing just that. And now, with all the rumors of war, it's time. David finished the last job, sold the other house and locked us away."

"But then..."

"Yes. He was shot. By that awful man wearing glasses."

The memory of the nose piece I found on the bus floor flashed like a neon sign. "Is his name Gary?" I asked, scarcely breathing.

"Gary?" She shook her head. "I don't know a Gary. It was the awful one who smoked cigarettes. He kept coming here making demands. I was scared of him."

"Did David know him?"

She nodded. "He helped David in the past. David paid him money. I don't know why he chose to attack us again."

"Was the money for a job to help gather some items?"

"Yes. Precious artifacts that might have been lost forever."

"I understand," I said. "Uh, just one second, okay Alice? I think I left the front door open. Let me go check."

Her eyes widened like the thought concerned her.

I hurried up to the top of the stairs, dialing on the phone as I went.

"Yellow," Uncle Chris answered in his usual corny way.

"Uncle Chris, it's Stella. I need you to come to the Brown house as soon as possible."

"Are you okay? Should I bring the police?" He must have heard the tension in my voice.

I thought about the frail woman. She'd have to face the police sooner or later, but maybe it would be kindest to break her in slowly.

"Just come by yourself. And when you enter the house, do it quietly. Everything is fine, but I have a nervous witness."

"What?"

"I'm sorry, I really have to go. Just come."

I hung up and tiptoed back down the stairs. Alice still sat in the same chair. Her shoulders wilted forward, like she felt defeated.

"Alice, it's me again," I announced myself. This time I went down several steps and sat on one. "This must have been so hard for you to be alone when David died. How have you survived?"

She shrugged and her bony hands squeeze into tight fists. "It's been hard. Horrible."

"I can only imagine. I'm so sorry." I meant every word. The woman was thin and pale. It was obvious that she suffered. "I know David ordered groceries. How have you been eating?"

"Oh, I've been dipping into our stores. Sometimes I get fresh fruit."

"How do you manage that?" I asked.

"I go into the house next door."

"Do you mean Charlotte's house? How do you get inside?"

She nodded. "There's a tunnel that connects the two houses. I only do it if I'm in dire need."

"Do you go outside as well?"

"Sometimes at night. David always said to make sure it was dark out. There's a trap door through the room down here. It leads to the garden."

"Is it located behind a huge rhododendron bush?"

Her head bob confirmed what I'd seen for myself on Charlotte's video. The white figure disappeared when it rounded the shrub.

"I can see you guys were set to live here for a long while. What went wrong?" *I mean, other than Mr. Brown getting shot.* I wanted answers, but I wanted to be careful not to push her too far. I may have been the first person she'd spoken with since her brother died.

"I told you, that evil man became greedy. Always stalking us. He was trying to find a way in. I heard him arguing with David one day, telling him he knew the goods were in the house. That he'd better split them with him or he'd pay."

"And David didn't want to do that?"

Her expression of horror said it all. "No. We were protecting them. There's no way David would give something that precious to the likes of him."

"Do you know who the man was?"

Alice shook her head and my hopes plummeted. Then she said, "But I do remember David calling him by name one time.

26

W hat had Alice just said? That she heard the name of the man who killed her brother?

"What happened?" My chest tightened with excitement.

"Well, they were fighting something awful. Yelling back and forth, and the man flicked his cigarette at my brother."

"Really! What did David do?"

"He stood as straight as an arrow. I wondered if they were about to get into a fight. 'Sam,' he said. 'Sam get off my property right now.'"

Electricity jolted through my nerves. Sam Smith. I knew it. I remembered trying to follow him during the open house. He led Jennifer through the place like he was familiar with it.

"I suspected him the moment he took the key," I huffed.

"The key?"

"From the desk drawer. It was hidden under—"

"Under the fake bottom." She smiled. "I took it. It's for the door at the bottom of the property. I was frightened the man might come back."

"Oh." I was caught off guard. "I'm so sorry. You must have been terrified." I wanted to gather the poor woman in my arms for a hug. "Were you scared to leave here, Alice?"

"Leave here?" Her eyes widened. "I haven't left the home since I was a school girl."

I swallowed hard as a cold sweat broke over me. This poor, poor woman. I couldn't imagine what sort of circumstances she must have lived under to think that this lifestyle was normal. To have never left this house in all these years. I remembered Miss Dolly saying that the father removed the kids from school. Eventually, David Brown broached the outside world and found a career. But as soon as David was able, he became a recluse again himself.

I wondered about this family dynamics, how something like this could even happen. It was obvious to me that the original Mr. Brown was a controlling man, brainwashing even. The mother had left the father years ago and moved to Florida. She abandoned her family. But what if it was such a horrible situation there was nothing she could do? Things were different back then. She might have only escaped by the skin of her teeth.

"I'm going to call a friend, okay? I think she will help."

"A friend?" Alice asked.

I nodded and put in a call to Charlotte. She was small and gentle herself. I thought it would be a good icebreaker for Alice, knowing all the people that she would be exposed to in a very short time.

"You want another ten minutes to do another search?" Charlotte spouted immediately when she answered.

"No. Everything is okay. I'd like you to come over and meet someone. Come inside. We're downstairs in the bonus room," I said.

That sweet lady didn't even argue, but immediately said ok.

I reached out a hand to Alice. "Come with me. Come upstairs. It's okay. You're with friends."

Alice stared at my hand with wide eyes filled with trepidation.

"Come on. Let's go have some tea. I could use a cup," I cajoled.

Slowly she rose. She followed me up the steps just as Charlotte called my name from the front door.

It took another chunk of time—in which I introduced Charlotte, and Charlotte stood with a gaped mouth to see her real life Rebecca— but we soon had acclimated to one another well enough to move into the kitchen.

A short while later, Uncle Chris showed up like a bull in a china shop, completely disregarding my plea for quiet decorum. Of course, I realized why, given the way our phone call ended. By this point Charlotte and I had Alice sitting at the table while Charlotte—after a quick trip home for the ingredients—busied herself with making tea. I filled in Uncle Chris with all that had transpired and then he went downstairs to explore the secret room himself.

Alice was understandably nervous. Charlotte was much better at calming her down than I had been, and I almost felt like, under different circumstances, they could have been friends. Who knew? Maybe they still would.

When Uncle Chris reappeared, his face was expressionless. I did catch him patting his pocket for a cigar as he hurried outside to use his phone.

A short while later, the police arrived, but more importantly, a social worker was there. She seemed to know how to deal with Alice. It was an odd moment when they led her outside. Alice blinked like she hadn't seen the sunshine in forever. I suspected that was probably true.

Uncle Chris informed me that the next stop for Alice was the hospital where they would evaluate her overall health. As I watched them take her away, a train of detectives flooded past me and down the stairs to mark and take everything in for evidence. I was shocked when the van showed up to collect it. Apparently there were several rooms below ground, each one stuffed with old paintings, swords, journals, jewelry and much much more. The Brown family had been hoarding Nazi and World War II antiques for a long while.

"Do you think we can prove Sam killed David Brown?" I asked.

"Well, we have the nose piece and the granola wrappers. I kind of doubt there will be any fingerprints left on them though since they were exposed."

"What about the footprints we found?"

"They can check his shoes to see if there's a match."

"And the detectives can see if he has a rifle. Do we know if the bullet was kept as evidence?"

"That I don't know." He sighed.

Wait a minute, Charlotte had said the gun had gone off twice. "Maybe we can find a bullet. Charlotte thought it went off twice."

Uncle Chris lifted an eyebrow. "Talk about a needle in a haystack."

I remembered the chunk of wood missing from the trim. "And the soda cans! I'm sure there is DNA left on the cigarette butts."

"Could be."

"And Alice said that David paid Sam off. There might be proof of that transaction."

"Possibly, unless it was cash."

"That's true, but Sam got Lasik at that exact same time. Georgie mentioned that he flirted with her about how she was a perfect ten, and something about how he had eyes like an eagle because of the surgery. That might be where he met

Jennifer Barker since she worked there as a receptionist. So there's proof of extra money."

"Good job!"

"I feel like I just had so many questions answered. It was Alice who was shutting the curtains so she could move about unseen. She's the one who destroyed the lock box. And the cat followed her through the underground tunnel."

"You have a theory on how the thefts happened?"

"Yeah. I think when David took inventory and saw World War II memorabilia, he made sure that box conveniently disappeared. Obviously, Sam saw it happen, or maybe orchestrated the disappearance. Either way, he knew what David was up to. David paid him either to keep that knowledge a secret or to help."

"Well, I'm going to put a call in to the trustee. I imagine this will change how the house sale will go through."

I looked at the front of the house. "Dang. I was looking forward to getting this off my hands, but I was also looking forward to the commission."

"Maybe no commission, but you may have given that woman a chance at life. There isn't much better than helping someone get free." He clapped my shoulder. "And you're about to go through the same experience again."

My heart fluttered with excitement and fear. I knew who he meant. My mom.

27

My day ended with me heading down to the police station to give a statement. Absolutely one of my least favorite things to do.

The station in Gainesville was bigger than I expected and the parking around the building filled with police cars. It took me a little while to find an empty space, and even then I was two blocks down the road.

I grimaced as I locked the car, needing to use the restroom, and now I had a long walk to boot. The breeze lifted my hair from my coat collar.

Starting toward the station, I dialed one of my favorite people. "Charity!" I said when she answered. "Guess what! There's a chance that maybe some of the items stolen from you may have been found."

"Oh, Stella! That's wonderful news. Something that will

please Gladys and draw her out of her sour mood she's been in lately, I hope. I'm glad you called. I've been meaning to talk to you."

"What's going on?" The wind was brisk and grabbed my hair. I gathered it behind my ear and ducked my head to face the breeze.

"Dolly has spoken so kindly of you to everyone. I was wondering if you would be up for another visit. Perhaps you'd care to read to them? They love mysteries."

I considered it for a moment. It was new ground for me and another commitment to boot. Yet I remembered that warm satisfied feeling I had while getting to know Miss Dolly. There'd been a meaningful exchange between us, one I'd benefitted from myself.

Feeling slightly impulsive, I agreed. I had to hold the phone from my ear to muffle Charity's excited squeals. After making plans for the following week, we hung up.

I finally made it to the police station, but I had one more phone call to make to Georgie. After I came down the mountain and back into better cell service, my phone dinged with a missed text from her. She must have heard somehow about what was going on at the Brown house and wanted to know how I was doing. I knew how she hated to text and that was actually underlined by her stating she didn't want to disturb me but to please be careful.

"Georgie, it's Stella."

"Stella! Are you okay? What an ordeal!"

"I'm good. How did you find out?"

"Oh, we were at Oscar's, and it came over his police radio."

I'd forgotten about the scanner. I hoped Oscar wasn't worried. "Everything is under control. What do you mean we? Who was with you?"

"Just Frank and me this time. We were fixing some air leaks around his windows. You know, trying to winterize the place. Carlson was there to help us."

My heart filled with gratitude. "You guys are the best. Hopefully the rest of the family can step up to the plate now that we're reunited."

"Don't worry about that. We're glad to help." She paused for a moment and then blurted. "I don't know what's going on with Carlson. Have you talked with him lately?"

"What? Me? No. Well, just one time since I found out he went on a date." I walked around the flag pole. Above me, the flag snapped in the wind.

"A date?" She groaned. "Oh, no. He didn't."

"Yeah! He really did. He found her on some online site," I said.

"No, I mean I can't believe he listened to Frank."

"What do you mean?" Suspicion crept into my voice, and I stopped in my tracks.

Georgie sighed. "You might want to kill him once you find out."

"Find out what?" Now irritation filled my veins. I was

whipping through the whole negative emotion gamut like a picture flipbook.

"Well, a few weeks back he and Frank were having a guy's night. I guess Carlson was really bummed that he hadn't been able to get your attention yet, and he asked Frank for some advice."

"Okay...." The word dragged out. I was on pins and needles waiting to hear.

"Frank told him that some girls respond by getting jealous. He suggested Carlson hint about going on a date."

I swallowed. Turned around. Paced four steps and considered my options. He lied to me? "So it wasn't true?"

"No." she sighed. "That boy's dating life is drier than a desert."

I fumed out-loud. All the grief I'd gone through the last week? He did that just to catch my attention?

Well he caught it all right. "Thanks for letting me know. I'm at the station right now and need to get inside. I'll call you later after I process all of this."

"You got it. Go in there and take no names. Talk with you later."

I slid the phone into my purse and hobbled up the cement stairs. Just a few more days and this sucker comes off, I grimly reminded myself. Now what did that mean, Carlson wasn't dating? Was he really trying to make me jealous, or had Frank misunderstood. Maybe Carlson was trying to avoid me and needed a good excuse.

The thought made me queasy.

With that lovely feeling churning inside, I was distracted, and allowed myself to be led to a back room before I'd had a chance to visit the restroom.

Giving my statement wasn't a quick process this time. Sam Smith was arrested for the murder of David Brown, and the police were nailing down every bit of evidence they could get. They wanted to know all the details about the bus, the video of Alice that Charlotte had, the cigarette butts and pop can, even the crows.

That was interesting though. The police also shared that they suspected the crows were stalking Sam after he threw rocks at them at the grocery store. They had the store's security video to base that off of, and I remembered Charlotte telling me a story about it as well. Apparently, the crows bombed Sam's car every chance they got.

I had no idea that crows were so smart. Or so vindictive.

It also gave me the chills. Because if the crows were at the house, that meant Sam was also there, hidden and lurking in the trees. Even though it was all after the fact, I felt incredibly threatened. I was never leaving home without my pepper spray again. In fact, I'd seen a new one that, if deployed, sent a message to five people that you were in trouble. I needed to track that one down.

Finally, I finished my statement and hurried for the bathroom. One of the best sights known to mankind was an empty stall when it's really needed.

Relief! I turned and flushed. The motion knocked a package of tic-tacs out of my pocket and into the bowl. Instantly, a vision of over-flowing water sprang into my mind.

I started pleading with the toilet. "Oh, no! Please go down. Please go down. Please go down."

Thankfully, it disappeared with nary a clog. Relieved, I opened the door.

A pair of eyes stared at me and then quickly averted. Good grief! Someone had heard me begging a toilet to make it go down! And at a police station!

I knew exactly what she thought as she went into another stall, making it obvious she was avoiding mine. Words of defense dried up in my mouth. I washed my hands with red cheeks and hurried out.

The only thing on my mind was escape, with my face half covered with my hand. *Stella, you really did it this time.* My chiding was in full force when I bumped into someone. Startled, I looked up.

Carlson.

Oh great! Had he heard that whole thing? My cheeks burned hotly. I was so caught off guard I'd forgotten I wanted to act dismissive to him. To be honest, I didn't know how to act right now, other than wishing for one of those futuristic transporting beams. Beam me to Australia, Scotty!

I beamed away all right. I stumbled off of him and somehow twisted just enough to catch my funny bone against the sharp edge of the reception counter. My boot caught under my other foot and I tumbled head-over-heels, landing in the most indecorous position. Tears threatened my eyes at the searing pain.

"How ya doing, Hollywood?" Carlson asked, bending down to give me a hand.

"Not well," I answered through gritted teeth. I allowed him to help me up.

"You hurt your arm?"

"You noticed." I hobbled over to one of the chairs in the waiting area and sat down, wincing so hard I probably looked like I'd bitten a lemon in half. Thank goodness I didn't have a dress on, or I would have flashed the entire precinct my whole enchilada.

"That was some fall, but you sure looked cute while doing it."

I scowled at him.

"What? It's a compliment."

I slowly stood, feeling like my bones were creaking, and hobbled out the door. It was when I was outside on the steps that I realized my car was still two blocks away. Groaning, I limped down, hanging on to the handrail while my other arm screamed, "Fire!"

The sun was blistering in one of those odd autumn moments. I found a bench and took a seat to examine the damage.

He must have followed because a moment later he stood

next to me, moving so that his shadow shaded my face. "Better?"

The pain made me feel extra spiteful, and I wanted to let him have it. "You and your date make any more plans?"

He snorted and shook his head. "I have a confession," he said. "I'm an idiot."

"Tell me something I didn't know." I scowled.

"Yeah, well I'm a bigger one than even I realized. There never was a date. It was some hare-brained idea I came up with to get you jealous." He opened up his ham-sized hands and shrugged. "There. You know. I'm lame."

"And have no game." I finished.

He grinned. "Truer poetic words were never spoken. Anyway, I felt terrible about that, and the idea didn't work anyway. So, I'm sorry."

He squinted at me, and I was surprised to see him look a little self-conscious. The great macho Ethan Carlson? Insecure?

I thought about calling him by his first name to really punish him, but decided he'd suffered enough. "It's fine. Just don't do it again. In fact, if I find that you ever lie to me...."

"I'll hand you my handcuffs and let you lock me up." He grinned, a little flirty. Slightly too flirty, if you asked me, considering the situation. I huffed.

"Aww, your ankle looks a little bruised." He squatted down and the sun shot me in the eyes again. I shaded them as he reached for my foot. "If I didn't know better, I'd think you loved to wear casts."

I rolled my eyes. *No game,* my inner voice reminded me.

Gently, he manipulated my ankle. "Does this hurt?"

"No. I mean a little but not bad."

He leaned forward and checked my elbow. "Lost some skin here."

I stared down at the red patch. My pride had been so bruised, I hadn't even noticed.

"Come on, let me get you a soda."

"No, I'm—"

He was already heading toward the convenience store, walking in those monster steps of his. A few minutes later he returned with two pop bottles. Looking a little shamed-face, he held out a package of cream-filled chocolate cupcakes.

"Thanks," I said, feeling like giving him a flirty look. *How do you do this?* I swooped my hair back and to the side and blinked. A hunk promptly fell forward, hitting me straight in the eye. I flinched and wiped my watering eye before finally giving up and tucking the hair behind my ear. I didn't have much game myself, I was finding.

Carlson sat down with a heavy thump, making the bench squeak. He stared out at the horizon while he worked on opening the package. After shuffling out a cupcake, he handed it to me, then he took the remaining one. Together we took bites of the chocolatey-frosting-goodness-otherwise-known-as-heaven-on-earth. I may have even given an approving hum.

We chewed in silence and then he cracked open my soda. He held out his to do a cheers. "We've both been through a lot."

"Is that what we're cheersing to?" I asked, confused.

"No. We're cheersing to the fact that we're both here. We're alive, and I'm happy."

"You're happy?" I grinned.

He smiled back. I kid you not. He actually smiled. "Yeah. I am. Been like this for a while. Ever since a certain lady moved here from the west coast."

I shook my head. "I would have never known."

"No?" His eyebrows squeezed together. "I thought I was making it so obvious. Calling you Hollywood and all. Shot the guy that tried to kill you that one time. Stayed at the hospital guarding you all night."

"That was sweet," I said. "Thank you."

"You're the one that was confusing. I didn't know where you and—what's that dorky-looking guy's name? Ronald?—I didn't know where you two stood."

I smothered my smile at his not so subtle jab. "His name is Richie, and I can understand that. I wasn't ready for anything because my family had me in so much turmoil."

"I get that. But you're the hot pepper that whipped them all into shape."

I laughed. "I try."

"Hmm," he said, taking another drink.

"You like hot peppers?" I asked.

"I do. Happen to be my favorite food." His eyes twinkled as he studied me. "Listen, I've been meaning to ask you on a date."

"Oh, yeah?" This better be good. "Where?"

"I want you to come watch the rain with me."

I glanced at the sky where not even a cottonball-sized cloud was visible. "It's not raining."

"Not yet. But eventually it will be. And I want to have as many practice dates as I can until then."

"Practice, huh? How are we this complicated?"

Carlson brushed back my hair, his lips pulled in that smirky smirk he got when he was thinking he was all that. "Hollywood, we aren't that complicated. It ain't complicated. Now kiss me."

He cupped the back of my head and stroked my jaw with his thumb. Then he kissed me. Strong, with just the right amount of tenderness at the end. I gasped when we broke apart, with butterflies tickling inside like they would burst free to carry me away.

Just my luck, at that moment my phone rang. It was from Ashmount Penitentiary. Still feeling dazed, I broke away from Carlson to answer.

"Hello?" I said, trying to change gears. At this rate my mental clutch was about to burn out.

"Hello," said the female robot voice. "You have a phone

call from Vanessa O'Neil from the Ashmount Penitentiary. Press one to continue."

I pressed one with shaking hands. "Mom?" I cried.

"Stella! It's me! I wanted to see if you were available to pick me up tomorrow! They moved my parole hearing up and I've been released!"

I squealed in excitement and nearly dropped the phone. The only reaction from Carlson was a slightly raised eyebrow. "Yes! I'll be there! What time?"

"Six am. Is that too early?" I nearly wept that her sweet voice was filled with concern that it would be too early for me to finally, for the first time since I was five-years-old, get a chance to hug my mom.

"No, Mom. Not at all! I'll be there waiting! And you'll stay with me when you get out?"

"If that's still okay?"

"Yes! Of course it is! I can't wait to see you."

"Me either, sweetheart. I won't hardly sleep a wink. I know it will be odd and strange for you, but I'm so looking forward to building memories with you again."

"Me too, Mom. Me too."

The operator gave us the one minute countdown so we quickly said our goodbyes. My heart nearly burst when my mom said, "Stella, I love you. I'm going to do my best to make up for what you've lost."

"I'm okay, Mom," I shouted over the operator's last

warning. "You have nothing to do when you get free except to live your own hopes and dreams."

"You are my dream, sweet—"

The phone went dead. I stared at it for a moment, sadness blossoming at being so abruptly unplugged. But then I remembered, tomorrow!

"She's out in the morning, huh? Coming back to your place?"

I nodded. Memories of when I'd first moved into the little house flooded my head. Honestly, I had goosebumps, remembering my first night here, remembering how I'd almost turned right around and went back to Seattle. The moving truck had gotten lost, and I'd wondered what in the world I'd done.

Now I felt sick with gratitude that I hadn't left, like I'd been so tempted to do. I couldn't even imagine the magnitude of that mistake and what I would have missed out on, if I had. I'd gained so much, and even though it was all still messy, it was *my* mess.

My phone buzzed.

"You got a text," said Carlson helpfully.

Talk about Grand Central Station! I glanced at the phone, wondering if I could hide from it for a while.

It was from Georgie. —**I know you're probably burnt out from talking to people, so I thought I'd text. I don't know what Cecelia did, but Oscar finally agreed to tell me about Derek! Will you come with me? I'm so excited! I'm**

determined to figure out what happened to Derek if it's the last thing I do.

The sun was shining warm and sweet, but a chill pierced my heart as I read her words. I held the phone stiffly as the world fell away and all the good emotions I'd just experienced were replaced with a sick fear.

Unreasonable, I know. I couldn't explain what was going on. But I also couldn't deny it. My gut told me to say no, to run away, to pretend I hadn't read the question. Destroy the phone if I had to.

I never ignored my gut. I swallowed and typed back —**yes.**

Everything inside me screamed that answering yes was about to impact all the things I'd fought so hard for and finally had. But, I couldn't tell who was being threatened. Was it my mom? Dad? Oscar?

I stared at Carlson, and his eyes squinted questioningly at me. It was then I knew without a doubt that, ready or not, this time, I was in over my head.

Carlson winked at me. "Did you know I was a good gardener?"

My head whirled. "What?"

"I don't know who has you looking like that, but I'm about to take them outside and plant them like a Christmas tree." He rubbed my knee. "We're a team now, right? And I love gardening."

A small smile escaped me. I rested my hand on top of his. "All right, this time you can be my back up."

Immediately, his face scrunched into a frown. "Back up? Well, hold on there a minute. What do you mean, back up?" His chest inflated with a full argument, just waiting to let me have it.

I laughed and tucked the phone back into my pocket. Georgie needed some answers about Derek. Ready or not, mysterious death, here I come.

28

The End

Thank you for reading With Killer Views. Stella is about to leap into another mystery, this time to find out what really happened to Georgie's fiancé. She has no idea the impact it's going to have on her own life. Read it now in the next book—

Terror on Top

See the Flamingo with the cupcake? This story is a collaboration with Stella, Carlson and Georgie in the Baker Street Cozy Mysteries.

If you haven't had a chance to check out the Baker Street Mysteries, you can catch up with the following titles. And they all come with free recipes!

Baker Street Mysteries— Where Oscar and Kari are first introduced! Join Georgie, amateur sleuth and historical tour guide on her spooky, crazy adventures. As a fun bonus there's free recipes included!

Cherry Pie or Die

Cookies and Scream

Crème Brûlée or Slay

Drizzle of Death

Slash in the Pan

Here are a few more series to whet your appetite!

Oceanside Hotel Cozy Mysteries—Maisie runs a 5 star hotel and thought she'd seen everything. Little did she know. From haunted pirate tales to Hollywood red carpet events, she has a lot to keep her busy.

Booked For Murder

Deadly Reservation

Final Check Out

Fatal Vacancy

Suite Casualty

Angel Lake Cozy Mysteries—Elise comes home to her home town to lick her wounds after a nasty divorce. Together, with her best friend Lavina, they cook up some crazy mysteries.

The Sweet Taste of Murder

The Bitter Taste of Betrayal

The Sour Taste of Suspicion

The Honeyed Taste of Deception
The Tempting Taste of Danger
The Frosty Taste of Scandal

Made in the USA
Columbia, SC
19 August 2020

16859081R00140